OF MOUSE AND MAGIC

OF
MOUSE
AND
MAGIC

ALLAN R. GALL

Two Harbors Press
Minneapolis, MN

Two Harbors Press

212 3rd Avenue North, Suite 290

Minneapolis, MN 55401

612.455.2293

www.TwoHarborsPress.com

www.ofmouseandmagic.com

ISBN-13: 978-1-936401-78-9

LCCN: 2011930199

Distributed by Itasca Books

Cover Artwork by Anne K. Welles

Typeset by Sophie Chi

Printed in the United States of America

ACKNOWLEDGMENTS

Thank you to my grandchildren, Zack, Danny, and Tommy, who asked me to tell them stories. Danny asked me to write this particular story when I didn't have time to finish the telling of it, and he drew the illustration of Rachel and Manny at the garden fence. Tommy was tucked under my arm as I sought a subject and seemed small and vulnerable, like a mouse, facing the unknowable, unforeseeable, fun, difficult, and confusing choices that make a life. Tommy also drew the map of Farmer Frank's farm. And Zack inspired me by saying the first draft was better than Harry Potter at a time when Harry Potter was his passion. Zack also made valuable editorial comments. Thank you to Akash, the voracious young reader who gave me confidence that the book was a good read. And thank you to my writing colleagues, Gene, Sarah, and Kristin, who gave me helpful editorial comments and affirmation that I was a writer. Thank you to my daughter, Anne, for her suggestions and encouragement and for painting the cover. And especially, thank you to my wife, Carmel, whose encouragement, patience and help through the nurturing of this project over the years made this book possible.

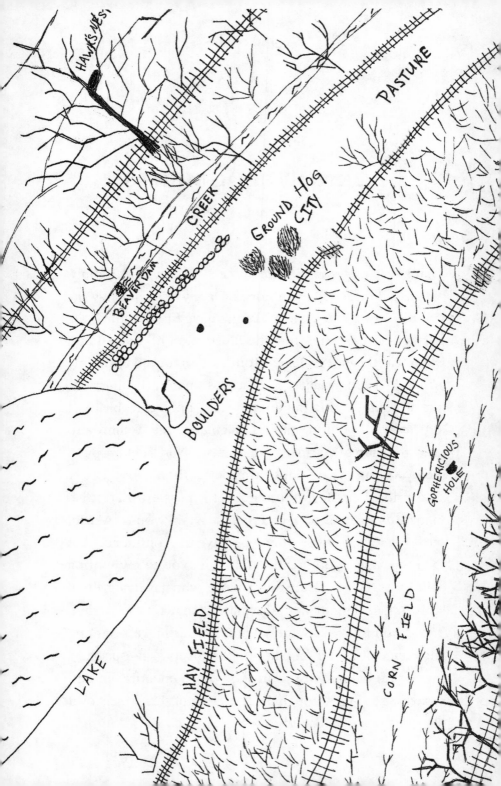

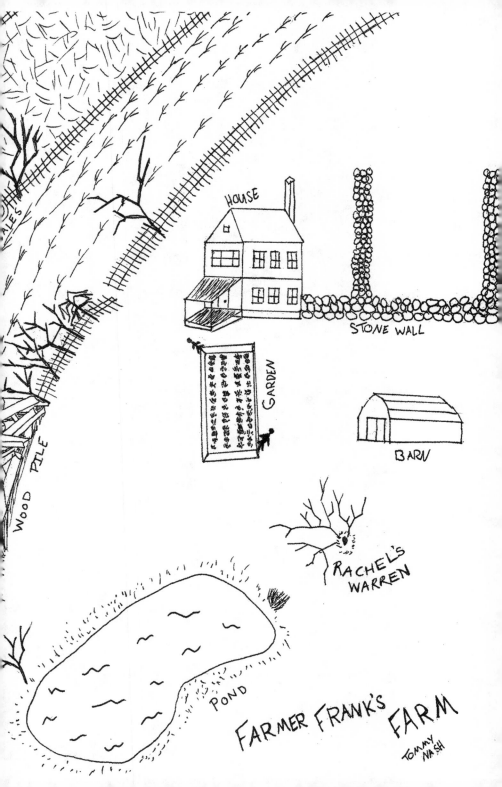

1. Imagination

Manny did not mind being born blind. All mice are. He had a full stomach, a warm nest, and no need to see. Manny was born in the woodpile that lay next to a fence on Farmer and Mrs. Frank's farm at the base of the Blue Ridge foothills.

Many mice lived in the woodpile, which they entered through a narrow passage formed by warped boards that led deep inside and kept out predators that hunted mice. At the end of the passage, a large knothole was their door down to a hollow tree-trunk that formed a hallway in the center of the woodpile among its boards and branches. From there, paths led throughout the woodpile.

The nest where Manny was born lay among rotted wood in the center of the woodpile and near the soil, where the earth kept it warm in winter and cool in summer. At the time of Manny's birth, it was early spring and still cold.

Manny's mother, Martha, was proud of the nest, proud of its wool lining from a sock the wind had torn from a clothesline. On the night Martha found it, her husband,

Fred, thought it was too dangerous to drag it to the woodpile. "A white sock? We might as well yell, 'here we are!'"

"We'll have it home in no time," Martha said, knowing that it would take all night. And the sock proved too thick to pull between the warped boards that were their entrance to the woodpile. They had to chew it in pieces small enough to carry down through the knothole and on through the rotted wood in the heart of the woodpile to their nest. They shared half of the sock with their neighbors, Louise and Macon.

At the moment of her children's births, Martha snuggled into the warmth of the wool as the first of her six babies— three girls and three boys—entered the world. All of them were tiny, but the last one was an itsy bitsy little thing. Martha pulled them close to her and whispered, "Each of you is special."

Fred looked at the babies, proud and happy to see that they all looked healthy, except for the last-born, who looked not so much unhealthy as just way too small. Fred stroked the few strands of white hair on his chin and furrowed his brow. He felt sure the smallest-born would not survive, but he did not say anything about that to Martha. To her he said, "Fine looking mice; I hope they grow up to be like you."

Their neighbor, Louise, spread the news of the babies and returned with other neighbors to congratulate Martha and Fred.

"What adorable babies," said one.

"Absolutely beautiful," said another.

"They couldn't help but be beautiful with a mother like Martha," said yet another.

Fred was thinking that everyone knew mouse babies were not beautiful. They are born a strange pink color with no hair and with their eyes closed. But he did not say anything.

Martha watched each of her babies intently for several days until she knew what she would name them. The first-born was chubby and always hungry; she named him George. The second-born she called Alvin, because he wore a perpetual mischievous grin. He would be trouble.

One of her three daughters had a slightly darker nose than most mice, a busy nose intent on every fragrance that found its way into the nest. "I will call you Bouqueet," Martha said.

The second daughter kneaded everything she came in contact with, as though studying the world through her paws. Martha named her Caressa. The third daughter she named Shyleen. She was the smallest of the girls and content to stay next to her mother.

Martha saw that the last-born, the extra tiny little mouse, looked fragile to others. But she felt the wiry toughness in his frame that said he would be strong for his size. Even when he slept, his eyelids fluttered, as though he were not deep in sleep, but thinking, learning. "You'll need every bit of your strength in this dangerous world," she whispered to him. "I will call you Manny."

* * *

Within a few days of his birth, Manny's life changed. He could see light. It was faint the first day, revealing only fuzzy outlines of things. But the next day, he could see his parents, the wool of their cozy nest, the opening that led to the world awaiting him, and his brothers and sisters. He saw that his siblings were starting to sprout gray hair.

He did not notice that he was small. Even when a neighbor commented that one of the babies was tiny, Manny did not realize she was talking about him. He thought of himself as big and strong. The world he heard the adults describe sounded more exciting than dangerous. He could hardly wait to see it, to experience its wonders, to feel its excitement.

The next change was that his parents began to take his siblings with them one by one to forage for food. "It's dangerous out there," their father said. "If you don't know what you're doing, you won't last two days."

"When can I go?" asked Manny.

"Soon," said his father, trying not to show his fear for Manny's safety outside the nest.

"But everyone else gets to go."

"And you will too."

His brothers, George and Alvin, sometimes said things like, "You'll never grow up. You're too small. You'll be caught your first time out."

But Manny did not listen to them. In *his* mind, he wasn't an ordinary field mouse, small and vulnerable. He fantasized that he could grow up to be a magically powerful mouse who protected the weak and administered justice to any and all who harbored a thought to harm a mouse—particularly to those with a mind to eat a mouse.

Manny's favorite pastime in the nest was listening to the conversations between his father and their neighbor, Moses. Moses visited often. He was lonely since his wife failed to return to their nest earlier in the spring. Of course, Manny's parents, Fred and Martha, never asked what had happened to her. When a mouse fails to return to its nest, everyone knows what it means. When Moses visited, he and Fred passed their time exchanging stories about their sightings of and escapes from the hunters of mice.

"Spotted a black-snake today down the fence by the turkey nest. I put distance between us in a hurry. Speed and endurance. That's what saved me today."

"You know the fox that lives toward the sunset? Caught sight of her yesterday from down wind. I think she may be expecting babies."

"Just what we need around here. More foxes."

"Maybe Farmer Frank will organize a hunt. My grandfather said he saw a fox hunt once. Men on horses with a bunch of dogs chasing after a fox. A grand sight, I'd say."

The more he heard, the stronger Manny felt that what the world needed was a magically powerful mouse to protect them from predators seeking their next meal. At the same time, his siblings' reports of their outings made him eager to leave the nest. George, in particular, often returned quite full of himself.

"You should've been with me," he said one day, "I went way down the fence-line; you wouldn't believe the kernels of corn I found."

"Mother and I found plenty to eat right next to the woodpile," said Shyleen, who was sure George was exaggerating. "I don't go any farther than I need to."

"Food, that's all you think of, George. There's more to life than eating. I intend to have fun," said Alvin, moving his ears up and down without moving his head—a trick he performed to get attention.

"Your idea of fun is not funny, Alvin," said Bouqueet. "You know what he did, Mom? He hid in the grass and rustled a dried weed as though there was an animal about to pounce on us when Caressa and I came past. We almost died of fright."

"It was just a joke, Mom. Even you would have laughed if you'd seen how high they jumped. If a real predator had been there, they'da been goners for sure."

"Scaring people is never funny, Alvin," said their mother.

"That's right. It wasn't a bit funny," said Caressa.

"I knew it wasn't a predator," said Bouqueet. "If it had been, I would've smelled it."

"Oh yeah, you think you've got a better nose than anyone," said Alvin. "Well, if it's so good, why did you jump?"

Listening to this, Manny was jealous, of course, but also excited at the experiences awaiting him, the experiences of every field mouse, and especially the experiences he imagined possible in the magic world of his daydream, where he was protected from harm and where he shielded other mice from danger. He could not wait for the chance.

To everyone's surprise, Manny's hair grew in with a crooked white mark across his chest that looked a little like a bolt of lightning and which Manny accepted as a sign that he really *would* become the magical mouse of his imagination. To his parents, however, it simply meant that he was ready to be taken into the fields. His mother said the thrilling words: "Okay, Manny, tonight I'll take you with me."

Manny followed his mother through the rotted wood along the path that led outside, barely able to breathe with excitement. The woodpile was rich in aromas. There was the decay of wood and leaves; the droppings of ants and other insects; the fragrance of oak, pine, cherry, locust, and persimmon trees; and the familiar smell of mice, the smell of his mother, his father, his brothers and sisters.

They moved slowly in the tall grass and weeds that grew along the fence-line until they came to a multi-flora rose thicket. "Watch out for the thorns," his mother said. "This plant is a safe hiding place, if you need it. It's almost impossible for anything bigger than a mouse to move among the thorny stems. Being small—all mice are small," his mother continued, trying to get her point across without revealing her concern that Manny was little, even for a mouse, "our size lets us get into places our enemies can't come, like these rose bushes and the woodpile. Don't ever lose sight of the woodpile. The woodpile is home, shelter, protection from the world."

Farmer Frank had started the woodpile many years earlier. Whenever there was a board, post, log, or tree-branch to be removed from somewhere, Farmer Frank added it to the pile. The wood from two of the original farm buildings was in this pile and the trunks and branches of every tree that had died. The result was a giant heap of boards, posts, tree trunks and branches visible from every part of the farm.

Manny stared at the woodpile. Framed against the light clouds in the sky that were passing its silhouette, the woodpile appeared to be moving away from them and toward the horizon. So when his mother finally said, "Let's go home now," Manny's heart jumped in his eagerness to catch up to the woodpile before it could slip away.

Every day, the family reviewed what the children had learned. Caressa reported on the textures of plants—how to tell them apart by how their leaves felt to the touch—milkweed, hogweed, wineberry, ironweed.

Bouqueet tried to describe the smells of plants, like honeysuckle, spicebush, sneezeweed, goldenrod.

Shyleen was cautious, choosing to stick close to her mother, and said little about what she was learning.

George had an eye for everything and anything edible: wild goosefoot, partridge berry, sassafras seeds, dogwood seeds.

And Alvin worried his parents by seeming not to take potential dangers seriously.

Each day's review of what the children had learned concluded with a lecture by their father. Today's was on snakes.

"Snakes," he said, tugging on the few strands of white hair on his chin as he always did when giving lectures, "have a mesmerizing power. If they catch you by surprise and you look up into their cold stare, you won't be able to take your eyes away. At least, I've never heard of a mouse who was able to do it. Caught in a snake's stare, a mouse is unable to move, terrified, standing as though its feet are glued to the ground, while the snake just comes closer and closer until it swallows them whole. It's not a pleasant thing to watch."

"I could eat a snake," bragged George. "If I find a dead snake, I'll drag it home, so you can all have a taste," he said to everyone but really directed at his sisters, knowing it would make them feel sick.

"George, you are so gross," said Shyleen. "Don't you ever think of anything except eating?"

"I have a better idea," said Alvin, moving his ears up and down. "We could drag the snake to the woodpile and watch everybody jump when they see it. That would be really funny to watch."

"Snakes are no joking matter," said their father. "You won't be thinking about what the snake tastes like or how to make a joke when you come face to face with one, I can tell you that. If you want to live long enough to eat and joke around, you'd better pay attention to these lessons."

Shyleen nodded her head in agreement and looked a little self-righteous with this intervention from their father.

Caressa, on the other hand, felt a rush of guilt as her father's gaze turned toward her. He'd caught her thinking she'd like to pet a snake. That snakes must feel completely different from anything else was exactly what she'd been thinking.

Manny was fantasizing that when he grew up, he might just stare the snake down, return the snake's gaze with unblinking intensity, open his eyes and mouth wider and more fiercely, and advance slowly and deliberately until the snake sensed that *it* was about to be swallowed whole. The snake would crawl away feeling sick at the thought of swallowing anything whole ever again and die of starvation.

"Time for bed," said Martha.

"Tell us a story, Dad," said Shyleen.

The story was called, "Zeus Saves the Day." It was their favorite. The story had several plot variations in which a young mouse would get caught up in what he was doing—following his nose or eating, running or resting—and be distracted from the dangers around him long enough to be facing death. The setting was always the hour before daylight when night was day and day was night, a mystical and dangerous time when Zeus, a mouse with magic powers, would appear.

Zeus did not always save the mouse through magic, though. Instead, he often appeared simply to remind the mouse of a practical skill or trick the mouse could use to escape, like when to run, which direction to go, how to move silently, when to hide, where to hide, when not to move, how to blend into the surroundings. The children knew all the variations by heart, but the near-death feature of each adventure made them hold their breath anyway.

"Time for a lullaby," said Martha when the story was finished.

"I'm too old for lullabies, Mother," George grumbled, but, as usual, he fell asleep in the middle of Martha singing:

> *Sleep, sleep tight, my little mice,*
> *Sleep, on tummies, filled with rice,*
> *Filled, with weed seeds, oats and wheat,*
> *Filled, with raisins, berries sweet.*
> *Sleep, sleep sound, for one more night,*
> *Rest, prepare, for morning's light,*
> *Rest, for hunting, rest for fun,*
> *Rest, my children, wait the sun.*

Manny was the last to fall asleep, fantasizing about becoming a mouse with extraordinary power, a force to scare the mouse-eaters of the world such that they would cease to think of having a mouse steak, a mouse soufflé, or a mouse mousse. Those thoughts would be history. Mice would run and play without a care for what smell the wind brought or what sound or sight hinted danger.

He would be Zeus, Lord of Lightning, Titan of Thunder, with a jagged silver mark of lightning on his chest, carrying a magic rod of lightning and thunderbolts, omnipresent, watching everywhere at all times. And, of course, he would be omnipotent, possessing unlimited power, able to crack a snake like a whip until it begged for mercy and promised to become a vegetarian.

Whenever an instinct would arise in bird or beast to have a little feast of mouse, Zeus would appear with his chest puffed out and just look them in the eye. He wouldn't even have to say anything. Just look. And the offending party would lie, saying, "Begging your pardon, Sir. I just had this thought, you know, of how I might contribute to the greater well being of mice in the world. Maybe I could do something to contribute to their happiness: sing a song, perhaps. I know a few good cat jokes, heh, heh. Did you hear the one about the cat who got his claw caught in his ear while scratching for mites and fell on his butt?"

"Never mind," Zeus would interrupt—well aware the creature was lying. "Mice are doing quite well without your help. Just run along and tell your cat jokes to the dogs."

Zeus would speak quietly but carry a rod of thunderbolts.

2. A Celebration of Life

Manny followed his father, who was showing him the trees and bushes along the fence-line in both directions from the woodpile. Fred knew every tree, bush, vine and weed-patch along the fence: oak, sassafras, cherry, dogwood, pear, persimmon, and mulberry trees and spice and autumn olive bushes. "Each tree and bush provides us with food in its season," he said. "And Farmer Frank plants corn next to the woodpile. There's plenty to eat."

Suddenly, Fred stopped. "Looks like a mouse lying up ahead. It's not like a mouse to sleep in the open."

The mouse was lying motionless on dried leaves blown up against the fence. Fred approached and nudged it. "It's Macon. Looks like he reached the end of his time." Macon was Louise's husband, the neighbors to whom they had given half the wool sock.

"How do you reach the end of your time?"

"Nobody knows exactly. The body just stops working. This was Macon's fifth time around the seasons. Not many mice see the seasons through five cycles."

Fred noted the unmistakable teeth holes in the body and scanned the area for the culprit, spotting Farmer Frank's calico cat, Flora, about to pounce from behind a small bush. "Into the leaves! Don't move a muscle, even if she steps on you!"

Flora was mid-air as they dived under the leaves. She landed on top of where they were and began stomping around, trying to feel them under the leaves. She stomped and waited, stomped and waited. She watched for movement. She listened. The mice had to be under the leaves somewhere.

She stomped her left front paw down right on top of Manny. He lay absolutely still, trying to make himself Zeus, Lord of Lighting. How could he do it? It seemed easy enough to imagine; it seemed right at the edge of his grasp, as though he could do it, if he could just think of the right words or move the right muscle. But nothing happened. He held still, thinking of Zeus, but unable to *be* Zeus. Seconds passed.

Flora picked up her paw and pounced on another section of the leaves. She scratched around in the pile. The leaves flew up. She stomped on them. The wind rustled some of them. She stomped on them as they moved. She grabbed a leaf and flipped on her back. She kicked the leaf away.

The wind joined the game, throwing more leaves at her. She trapped some of them in her paws. She rolled over Fred and Manny. The wind was king. There were more leaves moving than she could put a paw on. She leaped in the air. She stomped on the ground. She rolled and jumped. She tired of the game and put her face to the wind and Farmer Frank's house.

Manny and Fred lay still for a long time. "She's gone," said Fred at last. "That was close."

"Why didn't she eat him?"

"Farmer Frank feeds her. Well-fed cats just like to play, and they play rough. We need to get Macon to the woodpile for a proper celebration. Run get help. I'll wait here."

Manny ran, wishing he could fly. Zeus would fly. He couldn't, but he could run fast. In a short while, he returned with his mother, his brother Alvin, and Macon's wife, Louise.

"Macon had a great life," Fred said to Louise as she sat beside Macon, not fighting her tears. "Only the best see the seasons cycle five times."

"I know," she said, without looking up from Macon's body.

"You boys help your father move Macon," said Martha.

They took turns pulling Macon by his tail, which felt undignified but was the easiest way to move him. It was hard going among the tall grass and weeds along the fence-line. When they reached the woodpile, they pulled him into the broad hallway of the hollow tree-trunk.

"This is the perfect spot for remembering Macon. Thank you for bringing him here," said Louise, trying to feel grateful, but only feeling sad.

"All the neighbors will bring food," said Martha. "Boys, spread the word. Girls, help me gather grass."

Dark came fast with the setting sun. It swallowed the day's warmth and bore cold on its back. But inside, the woodpile preserved a hint of the afternoon warmth and was still with the quiet of waiting.

All the mice who lived in the woodpile and many from farther away gathered that night to offer comfort to Louise. They sat near Macon's body and shared stories about him.

"No one else knew as much about plants as Macon did," observed one of his friends.

"That's right," said another. "We know the plants by sight and taste. But Macon had names for them. I remember once Macon talked about the seeds and leaves of a plant, using the name he'd given it. We all nodded, pretending to know which plant he was talking about, even though we didn't!"

Later, they took Macon's body to the top of the woodpile for the celebration of life. Everyone sat in circles around Macon's body. Moses, the oldest and wisest mouse anyone knew, stood next to Macon's body. The hair on his face had turned mostly white, making him look ghost-like as he addressed the circles, moving slowly around the body as he spoke.

"Fellow travelers in this circle of life. We are mice. We live off the bounty of the earth, and we are abundant. We are. Therefore, life is. Life is for living. We find joy in our life and accept its end. Death is also for life. We are here to commit Macon's body to the nurture of life. Life to death. Death to life. Please join me in the life-chant."

The chant began slowly, built only slightly in volume, and settled back into the throats from where it had started.

> *Spirit to body, body to spirit,*
> *to body to spirit, to body again.*
> *Life to death, death to life,*
> *to life to death, to life again.*

The celebration of life ritual was rare. Most mice simply disappeared, never returned. Their families were left to assume they had been caught and eaten. Finding a body hardly ever happened. So, for each mourner, it was a moment to remember Macon, but also to remember each of their friends and relatives who had not returned. A chant for all of the disappeared.

Moses gestured once more, "Peace to Macon. Peace to the creature about to receive the gift of his body. Let us go in peace."

The mourners did not linger. It was dangerous to be out in the open, especially in numbers. "What will happen to Macon now?" Manny asked his mother after most of the mice had left.

"Macon's body will disappear, but his spirit will always be with those who loved him. Love *is* the spirit, and it never disappears."

"Why are we leaving his body here?"

"Macon no longer needs his body. It will nourish another life."

Manny and his parents stayed with Louise after everyone else had left. No one said anything. They did not look at Macon's body. They did not look down the fence-line toward the trees where everyone at some time or other had seen the luminescent eyes of the raccoons or the dark forms of vultures, watching, waiting.

"I'm sorry Louise," Martha said at last. "It's not safe to stay with the body. Why don't you spend tonight with us?"

Louise agreed and went with them through the familiar passages and knotholes, along the path in the rotted wood, and down to Fred and Martha's nest. That night, Louise thought about the good times she and Macon had shared. One of their secrets was that Macon sang to her. He sang about the pains and difficulties of life, though he never sounded sad, and she knew that, even alone, she would never hear silence. The sound of blues would fill her black nights.

3. Rachel

Manny's father finally said it: "Tomorrow, you can hunt food on your own. Your mother and I have taught you what we can."

Manny did not hear the words exactly. What he heard was that he was free to be Zeus, Lord of Lightning, Titan of Thunder. He never hesitated. Mostly at night, Manny set out to experience everything: the changing weather; the smells and sounds of animals, trees, plants, birds, and insects. The world was beautiful, and every smell promised food. It was hard to believe it was dangerous.

Nevertheless, Manny prepared himself. One skill he practiced was running, preparing for the times when the ability to run far and fast might save him. He'd heard his father say it often: "Speed and endurance. That's what saved me today." He liked to run, and he ran in a rhythm that was effortless. And on this particular day, he ran toward an autumn olive bush next to a clump of three persimmon trees in the pasture east of the woodpile.

Stopped beneath the autumn olive bush and looking up to see if there was fruit, he heard the sound: the snap of a twig. He froze, hoping to smell what sounded quite close by. But the wind was blowing from the wrong direction. He whirled around and found his world reduced to a calico cat's green eyes. In one leap, Flora pinned him to the ground with her front paws.

Manny was too scrunched to squirm. The paws were warm, and the claws had pierced the dirt around him, leaving him without a scratch. It almost seemed safe. When Flora jumped back to see the prize under her paws, Manny lay huddled in a tight ball, remembering what his father had said. A well-fed cat might play with a mouse until it died, rather than eat it. He was about to be a toy! The survival skills of quick side-steps, pretending to be dead, and finding cover were not possible. What he needed was to become Zeus and teach this cat a lesson!

Flora pounced again, spearing him with her claw and flipping him into the air where a gust of wind cradled his small body and carried him for a surprising distance. His side felt as though it was ripped completely open, and he expected to land in a dead heap. Instead, he hit alive and hard between the autumn olive bush and the persimmon trees and rolled into a hole, turning once, twice, three times down the descending slope into the ground. Flora leaped to the spot where she had seen him land. It was a dark hole.

Inside the hole, Manny opened his eyes—surprised to be still alive. Above him, the light from the top of the hole dimmed as Flora thrust one of her paws in, reaching within inches of where he lay. His side was throbbing, but he rolled onto his feet and made his way farther down into the hole. He felt somewhat safe—at least from the cat. But whose hole was this? How would they feel about his coming in?

"Who's there?" asked a voice from below.

"It's me, Manny. I'm a mouse," said Manny, not sure he should have said that. What if the creature eats mice—or just likes to play with them until they die? The thought occurred to him that he should have said he was Zeus, wielding a rod of thunderbolts, but it was too late.

"Come on down. I'm Rachel. I'm a rabbit."

Manny continued down and made the last turn to where he faced Rachel. She had kind eyes, but she was huge. Her long ears and big teeth looked menacing. "Please excuse me. I didn't mean to barge into your home. I was flipped in here by a cat. If you don't mind, I'd like to stay until the cat leaves."

"Of course. Welcome to my home. My, you are a small little mouse, aren't you? What's wrong with your side? You're bleeding. Let me have a look at that." Rachel spoke softly, noticing that Manny appeared frightened of her. "It's not too bad. But I imagine it smarts a bit, doesn't it?"

"Yes, it does. It hurts really bad."

"I keep some foam flower weed here that helps heal cuts. Let me chew up a paste to put in that wound of yours." Rachel put some of the foam flower in her mouth and chewed it. "Hold still. This will sting a bit. What did the cat look like?"

"It had orange, black, and white patches and huge green eyes. And her breath smelled bad."

"That would be Flora, Farmer and Mrs. Frank's cat. Comes out here a lot. Well fed and slow, really. She'll wait at the top of the hole for awhile. We may as well have lunch and a nap." She went to the far corner of the warren and brought back two carrots. The smaller one was as big as Manny.

"These carrots are fresh. I got them a few nights ago."

"Thank you. They smell delicious. What did you call them?"

"They're carrots. Good for your eyes, my mother said. Seem to be pretty good generally as far as I can tell."

"My parents never told us about carrots," Manny said with a questioning tone.

"Well, parents can't think of everything. Most of what we learn, we learn on our own—sometimes from making mistakes. I've made a few myself, like this place on my right hip where there's no fur. I got that from some barbed wire once. You can lie down right over here," she said, as she puffed up a small mound of grass.

"I don't mean to be any trouble."

"Oh, it's no trouble at all. I like having visitors."

Manny put his head down, wishing his mother were there and fantasizing that he was the all-powerful Zeus with a magic rod.

* * *

In Manny's dream, Zeus leaped between a mouse and a cat and jabbed his magic rod into the cat's open jaws just as it was about to sink its teeth into the mouse. The cat couldn't close its mouth. It leaped around in agony.

"Promise you will never eat another mouse, and I will release you," said Zeus.

But the cat couldn't answer with the rod in its mouth. Instead, it nodded its head to say yes as best it could, and Zeus pulled his magic rod out. The cat held its sore jaw and looked in amazement at the little mouse. "Who are you?"

"I am Zeus, defender of mice, friend of the good, foe of evil."

"But I'm not evil. I'm just hungry."

"You will not go hungry. There's much to eat in the world. But I am putting this hex on you. From now on, you will not see mice as a source of food. They will not smell good to you, and you will not want to eat them."

"Thank you," said the cat, not sure why she was saying that.

"You are most welcome," said Zeus, staring intently at the cat to see if she was being sincere and to send a message that it would be in her interest to be so.

Anne Welles & Dan

4. Farmer Frank's Garden

"Wake up, Manny," said Rachel. "Flora will have left by now. I'm going to Farmer Frank's garden. Why don't you come with me?"

Manny thought he should go home, but he felt disoriented in the warren and unsure of the direction of the woodpile. And he did not think he should stay in Rachel's home while she was gone. It was so big it looked as though many creatures that eat mice could come in and find him. "Okay, I'll come with you."

Following Rachel in the moonlight, Manny could see that her hair was turning white, and she hopped with a hitch in her hip—the one with the scar. She was an elderly rabbit. Still, even running as fast as he could, he fell behind.

In the lead, Rachel was thinking that circumstances were not the best. The three-quarter moon was high and white. She was not exactly afraid, but for a moment, she longed to be the brazen rabbit of her youth when she bore more disdain than fear for Farmer Frank and his dog. "You okay?" she asked, looking back for Manny. "The garden is not much farther."

The going was hard, but relatively safe. The field was unmowed, providing generous cover until they came to a freshly mowed strip between them and the garden. Here, they stopped and sat among the last of the tall grass and weeds, looking toward the garden fence. Two scarecrows were mounted on two of its posts, one directly in front of them, and the other at the far end of the garden. From Manny's vantage point, the fence appeared to rise half-way to the white sky, forming a horizon separate from that of the earth.

"The dangerous part of the journey lies ahead," said Rachel, stepping to the edge of the weeds. She sniffed the air. She turned her ears in all directions. "It's clear."

Manny was using his nose too. The night air sharpened all the smells. He was still learning which smells said "safe" and which said "danger."

"You're small. You can enter the fence anywhere you want," said Rachel. "I get in through a hole I dug under the fence. It's this way."

Although it was true that the fence posed no obstacle to Manny, from his perspective, it was a frightening barrier that warned, "Don't cross me. Whoever trespasses here will suffer. Fences are signs."

"Are you sure it's safe to go through the fence?" he asked.

"Of course, it is. Farmer and Mrs. Frank are asleep, and their dog, Rusty, is old. I think he's decided to share the carrots. Why not? He doesn't eat them."

"Where is the dog?"

"He sleeps in a box on the porch of the house. Let's go."

They walked along the fence to where Rachel's hole under the fence should have been. Rachel stopped. Something was wrong. The hole should have been right there. She looked up. Yes, she was right below the post with the scarecrow. It had a straw hat and an oversized, loose blouse, and it pivoted on a broom stuck into two metal loops. It moved with the slightest breeze and looked alive.

"Don't worry," said Rachel, seeing Manny's anxious glance at the scarecrow. "She's not real."

Rachel studied the ground. The hole should have been right next to the base of the post. Some weeds had been growing there, and they hid the hole. Now the weeds were gone, and so was the hole. *Farmer Frank must have pulled up the weeds and found the hole*, thought Rachel.

Rachel did not like the look of it. For a moment she thought to retreat. One instinct pushed her toward the smell of lettuce and carrots in the garden. Another held her back. "Something is not right," it said. "Something has changed. Something has happened to what was known and safe."

Rachel was not young and foolish. But she also did not accept that she was too old to challenge obstacles to what she wanted. She felt the rush of youth as she considered what she knew she would do. She would breach the fence again. She would slip into the garden and eat as much lettuce and as many carrots as she wanted. She started to dig.

"I thought you had a hole here?" Manny asked anxiously.

"I did," Rachel replied, trying to sound unconcerned, as though finding the hole closed was expected, routine.

"So, why are you digging a new one?"

"I'll be inside the garden in a minute. Crawl through the wire."

"Okay," said Manny, but he waited. He did not feel he should enter the garden before Rachel. The fence still seemed like a barrier that was not meant to be crossed. Wasn't that the purpose of the scarecrow? To warn them to stay out?

The scarecrow's face was the mask that Mrs. Frank had worn to a costume party the night she had met Farmer Frank when they were young. It was the mask of a blond movie star, Marilyn Monroe, and it smiled invitingly—or maybe sadly. Was it happy? Or was it laughing at them? Manny felt the smile was directed right at him, and he could not take his eyes off her. A breeze grabbed the blouse and the broom, moving the scarecrow one direction and then letting her turn back again, leaving her blouse and skirt hanging still and her face resting its smile on Manny. Was the smile friendly? Or was it a lure to certain death in the garden?

Rachel dug quickly. The dirt flew out behind her. "I'm in," she yelled, breaking Manny's trance. "What are you doing outside the fence? Follow me. The lettuce is over there."

Manny stepped back from some of the taller plants to get a better view of Farmer Frank's house. It stood just beyond the far end of the garden. Reflecting the moonlight, its windows were the dozen eyes of a watchful, living creature. Manny's head moved slowly back and forth as he watched it, making the house appear to sway, as though breathing. He shuddered. "I don't see a dog on the porch. I thought you said the dog slept on the porch?"

Rachel looked up at the empty porch. "Well, I'll be. Rusty's gone and so is the crate where he slept. He was getting old. Maybe his time came."

Rachel felt sad. Not that Rusty was exactly her friend, but his presence told her that everything was the same. She'd eat what she wanted and be gone. Suddenly, the night wind felt cold. "We need to keep moving," she said in a tone more confident than she felt. Something was changed. Something was wrong.

Hopping toward the lettuce in the garden, Rachel passed some dog poop. It did not smell familiar. *Rusty must have eaten something different today*, she thought.

Running to catch up with Rachel, Manny's fear passed. He bounded forward, springing from one dirt clod to another, barely touching them in his speed, pretending he was Zeus, leaping from tree to tree, from house to house.

"Just taste this lettuce," said Rachel, as Manny caught up. "It never gets better than this. Old farmer Frank is one of the best. The lettuce is as sweet as honey."

Manny tasted the lettuce. It was definitely sweet. But as he ate, he started to sense that his nose was not happy with it. What started out smelling fresh and delicious was suddenly filling his nostrils with a strange smell bearing no resemblance to the taste of the lettuce—no, not strange, but rotten, the awful garbage smell of dog breath! Dog breath? Manny looked at the lettuce in his paws, trying to make sense of it. Dog breath? How could lettuce…? "DOG BREATH! DOG BREATH! DOG BREATH! RACHEL, RACHEL, THERE'S A DOG COMING!" he shouted.

Even as she heard Manny yell, Rachel was already in motion. *Oh no, oh no, what have I done*, she thought. *I got careless. Why wasn't I paying more attention? How could that old dog be coming so fast? There's no way Rusty can run like that.* And then she heard the growl and the high-pitched bark. It was not Rusty's voice, not the voice of an old dog. It was a young dog moving fast. Suddenly, everything made sense.

Farmer Frank has a new dog! How could I have been so careless? she thought. *The signs were all there. My hole under the fence was closed. Rusty wasn't in his usual spot. The dog poop didn't smell right. I've been coming here all my life, and now I could die here. Well, not if I can help it. Young dog or no, he'll need to be a quick and smart dog to catch me.* But that was the young Rachel thinking. A sharp pain shot from her bad hip on the initial push-off. The dog was almost on her, and she could see the outline of black spots on white. Dalmatian! *Oh my God, there could be a hundred more where that one came from*, she thought.

In a dead heat to the fence with a Dalmatian, Rachel knew she did not stand a chance. She took a sharp left and leaped over one of the rows of sprouting lettuce. It gave her a brief advantage, but not enough. She cut back across more rows of sprouting vegetables again and again. Around one more corner and under a wheelbarrow that she saw just in time to lower her ears.

The Dalmatian didn't see the wheelbarrow in time—or misjudged it. He swerved, but slammed his hindquarters against the handles, knocking it over. He yelped and lost his stride—just enough for Rachel to gain a few steps.

All the while, Manny was watching and praying to turn into Zeus, Lord of Lightning. He wanted so badly to save his friend Rachel, and he could not see how to do it. If he were Zeus, he'd leap between them, wave his magic rod, and turn the dog to stone. Or maybe it would be more fun to punch the dog straight away in the nose until it turned tail and went howling off in the opposite direction.

Rachel cut another quick turn and was coming back to where Manny was watching with little distance separating her from the dog. Manny did not hesitate. He leaped into the gap between them, facing the dog as though he really *were* Zeus, Titan of Thunder.

The dog was so shocked, he threw his front legs out in full braking position, simultaneously swooping his head down toward the ground to snap little Manny between his teeth. But the move wasn't that smooth. Manny held his ground only for the instant it took for the dog to throw his feet into braking mode. As the dog's front paws plowed into the dirt on either side of him, Manny threw himself to the side. The dog's paws sent dust and clods of mulch flying. One clod clipped Manny's hind legs and sent him tumbling.

The dog's tongue swooshed past, spattering Manny with drool and sending a wave of moist, hot air over him as he held his breath, trying not to smell it. DOG BREATH!

Manny recovered and ran straight under the dog in the opposite direction, burrowing under a large clump of mulch. By the time the dog flipped himself around, Manny was out of sight. The dog paused. Where was the mouse? Or was it the rabbit he wanted? Manny was so close to the dog, he could feel the heat of its body. The dog gathered his nose, let out a howl, and took off after the more interesting prey—the running rabbit. Rachel still had a ways to go to reach her hole under the fence.

CRASH! The door of the house flew open and Farmer Frank appeared in his pajamas with his shotgun. "What's going on out here?" he yelled. "Dal!? What ya chasin' there? Nasty varmints. A man can't even grow a few vegetables in peace any more." Boom! He fired the shotgun up in the air out over the field.

Rachel did not pause, but the dog did. He was unsure what he was supposed to do. The gun was new to him. He stopped and looked back at Farmer Frank, panting happily with his tongue hanging out. Obviously, his job was finished.

On the other side of the fence, breathing heavily, Rachel looked back toward the house. Rusty was standing beside Farmer Frank. *That's great,* thought Rachel. *The farmer is letting old Rusty sleep in the house now.* Rachel felt good. There was change, but Rusty was still there. And she had escaped again.

She looked carefully at the new dog. His coloring was not quite right. The white was a little yellow; the spots were too big and more dark brown than black. *He's not a real Dalmation*, she thought. *He's a mongrel, just like Rusty. It all kind of fits. Farmer Frank raises more vegetables than he needs and doesn't want to share them. If he needs a dog, he saves one from the pound. But what does he need a dog for? Is the dog supposed to keep other animals from eating the stuff Farmer Frank doesn't need? What's the point of that? Maybe it's all show? Maybe Farmer Frank just wants a dog for a friend? The dogs seem to like him.*

From under the mulch, Manny heard the soft rustle of Rachel's escape through the radishes and cucumbers to the hole in the fence, but he stayed hidden with his heart pounding so loud he was sure the dog could hear it. He waited until he heard the dog running back to the house. Then, he crawled out from under the mulch and walked to the fence, unseen and unheard.

Rachel was waiting. "That was the bravest thing I've ever seen."

"I was Zeus," said Manny, smiling. But inside, he didn't feel brave. He just felt tired. He felt his legs could not carry him another step.

"We have to hurry," said Rachel.

"Hurry? I can't even move. I need to sleep."

"If you do, you'll wake up in a predator's mouth. I guarantee it."

"But my legs hurt."

"Sooner or later we all run for our lives. Run when you think you can't and you'll live to run again. You saved my life; I'm not going to have tonight be the end of yours."

Manny looked up at the scarecrow. A faint breeze made her head nod as though she were saying it would be okay for him to come back. Farther away, the house now bore the moon on its roof. The reflected light was gone from the windows, and its life was still in the night air. He started to run. It hurt. He ran anyway.

5. Courage and Craft

Manny was running fast for a mouse, slow for a rabbit. Rachel worried. The mowed stretch from the fence to the high grass and weeds was a short distance, but in that pre-dawn moment, she felt as though they would never reach the tall grass and weeds that offered protection.

"It's not far," Rachel said to encourage Manny. Thinking about what had happened, Rachel wondered if she had handled the garden incident right. *Maybe she had panicked. The dog might not have hurt her. He probably just wanted to chase her. After all, he was almost certainly well fed. And he was barely more than a puppy. He would have chased anything that moved. Maybe she should have stood her ground and said, "Have a carrot Mr. Dog. They're good for your eyes. And lettuce is good for the bowels. Your poop doesn't smell too good."* She laughed thinking about it.

Manny ran on the excitement of what had happened in the garden. True, he had not turned into Zeus, but he had done a courageous thing. He had used his real skill at quick movement and hiding to save himself and his friend Rachel.

They had almost reached the weeds when the pounding of the air closed in on them. Rachel's big ears picked it up first. She whirled around just in time to see the owl bearing down. "Look out," she yelled.

Manny turned and looked up at the sky where the owl's wings carried the bird toward him. Two large, unblinking brown eyes, suspended from wings, were focused on the tiny field mouse without emotion or mercy. The wings stretched taut and went silent as the eyes dived for the kill.

Scrunch! A great weight landed on Manny, pushing him flat into the ground. But instead of the talons he expected, the force was a warm, fur-covered body. "Keep down," yelled Rachel from on top of him.

Thud! Manny felt another jolt. The owl had dived into Rachel with its talons. But it was a barn owl, too small to pick Rachel up. The talons gripped her body and tore away some fur and skin, but Rachel stayed fast to the ground.

"Are you okay," asked Rachel.

"Yes. What happened?"

"The owl dived for you, but I was more than she could carry. She's circling for another run at us. Grab the fur up by my chest, and hang on."

Rachel leaped forward just before the owl struck again, trying to hit low toward the front where Manny was holding on. Rachel swerved and took the hit in her side. The owl pumped her wings, but her talons came away with only a little fur and skin.

If I were Zeus, Manny was thinking, *I'd just grab those talons and hold the owl to the ground until it flapped to exhaustion.*

He was holding onto Rachel with the same determination. When the owl made her next pass, Rachel faked a pause and leaped long. The owl's talons grazed Rachel but did not get a grip.

One last hop and Rachel was in the tall weeds of the unmowed pasture. "Quick, Manny," she said, "find cover."

Manny dived under a thick bunch of dried stalks. "The sun will be up soon," yelled Rachel. "When the owl leaves, follow my scent; I'll wait for you back at my warren."

Manny stayed hidden and absolutely still. He listened to Rachel running through the weeds until the sound of her footsteps was gone. The owl circled the area once, twice, three more times. Manny barely dared to breathe. On the fifth pass, Manny heard the wings pause. Was she diving? Had she seen him? The owl came in low and close. Manny felt the air stirred by her passing, but she did not see him and continued on.

Manny wanted nothing more than to put his head down and go to sleep, but he remembered what Rachel had said about waking up as somebody's breakfast. He tracked Rachel, moving slowly, carefully, too tired to run. The ground was covered with stalks that he had to crawl over and under, making his progress slow and difficult. What was needed was Zeus to swoop down and carry him back to the safety of the woodpile. The woodpile. Manny wondered if he would ever get back to it. He had only been gone a day and a night, but it seemed much longer.

The smell of the autumn olive bush reached Manny before he saw the entrance to Rachel's warren, and he exhaled the tiredness in his bones with the relief of finding this familiar landmark. "Rachel, are you there? It's me, Manny."

There was no answer. Manny hesitated. Should he continue on down? What if Rachel was not there? What if a predator had eaten her and was still there? He rounded the next turn and called in a hoarse whisper, "Rachel, it's me, Manny," not sure he wanted to be heard.

Peeking around the last corner, he saw Rachel lying on her bed of grass with her eyes closed. Her wounds were matted with blood. He looked around and saw the foam flower Rachel had used on his wound. He chewed some into a paste and pressed a little into each wound. Rachel flinched.

"Rachel, it's me, Manny. Can you turn onto your other side?"

Rachel struggled, and Manny pushed to help her turn over. He put the paste in every wound. "Is there anything else I can do?"

"Bless you," moaned Rachel. "The paste feels good. I just need to rest." She closed her eyes.

What should he do now? Manny did not have time to think about it. A barely audible sound from the entrance shaft told him that another animal was entering the hole. Manny looked around for a place to hide. There was nowhere, really. The animal's smell was familiar and not threatening. It smelled like Rachel.

"Hello. My name is Manny. I'm a friend of Rachel's. She's hurt," he called out so that whoever was coming would not be startled to find him there.

"Pleased to meet you. I'm Rebecca, Rachel's daughter," said the rabbit who appeared. "What happened? How did mother get hurt?" She leaned in close to look at the wounds and gently smoothed her mother's fur near the wounds. "Nasty cuts. Did you put the paste in them?"

"Yes, your mother taught me. She treated a wound of mine. That's how we met. She got hurt protecting me from an owl."

"So, Mother took you to Farmer Frank's garden, did she?"

"Yes, how did you know?"

"It's the only place mother goes for food anymore. I worry she'll get careless as she gets older, or maybe just too slow, and fall to the dog's slobbery mouth."

"Oh, no," said Manny. "I saw Rachel in the garden. She's still fast. She got away from Farmer Frank's new dog."

"Farmer Frank has a new dog?"

"Yes. And he's young and fast."

"I'll warn everyone; anyway, I need to let my sisters and brothers know that mother is hurt. Would you stay with her? I don't want her to wake up, feeling alone. I won't be gone long."

In a hop, she was gone. Manny sat alone, watching Rachel sleep and wishing he could run as fast as a rabbit. It seemed to him that rabbits could run faster than the wind—as fast as Zeus. Manny closed his eyes, drifting off to his imagined, magical world where he was Zeus, floating lazily above the fields, keeping watch over the mice and protecting the woodpile. He was asleep in an instant.

When Manny awoke, the warren was full of sleeping rabbits, and he eased himself past them to get to the exit of the warren. He had been gone from the woodpile for two days and nights. He couldn't wait to tell his family about his adventures.

At the top of the hole, he looked, listened, and smelled to see if it was safe to return to the woodpile. A light breeze brought the smell of fox breath—the stench of dead mice. He scampered up the autumn olive bush to see how much time he had, how far off the fox was.

From the top of the bush, he could see a swaying path being cut through the weeds, outlining the silky movement of a fox. She was a considerable distance away, and the wind was favorable. The fox would not have smelled him or the much stronger scent of the rabbits in the warren.

He could easily escape. But unless something diverted the fox from her course, she would come upon Rachel's warren and the biggest feast of her life. Off to the west, was the clump of multiflora rose bushes on the fence-line. It was the nearest safe destination. He had a good lead on the fox. He could make it if he ran fast and the fox didn't see him right away. He needed the fox to chase him, if he was to save his friends, but not too soon, if he was to save himself. He ran. With every push of his legs, Manny could feel his muscles; he was Zeus, Lord of Lightning, Titan of Thunder, a blur of speed, a blaze of light.

When he felt he had enough of a head start, he ran up the stem of a pokeweed that stood high above the rest of the weeds and grass. From there, he would see the fox, and, he hoped, be seen. His weight shook the seed-laden top. It was a brittle pokeweed from the previous summer and rustled noticeably as he climbed. Manny saw the fox stop and turn its head in his direction just as the plant snapped, dumping him onto the ground.

The lure worked. He could hear the swish of the fox moving toward him through the weeds. He ran possessed. He leaped off every footing without seeming to touch anything. The multiflora rosebush was very close, but the stench of dead mouse breath was bearing down on him like warm wind advances a tropical storm. *Zeus, Zeus, please can I be Zeus,* thought Manny, pushing his legs one last burst as he dove into the thicket of the multiflora with the fox's stinking hot breath warming the hair on his back.

The fox dived part-way into the bush but jerked back in fear. She was no stranger to the thorns of the multiflora rosebushes and was not about to take one in the nose. But she was also not about to give up on such a tender breakfast. She lunged and pulled back and lunged again, trying to scare Manny into making a run for it. But Manny only moved as much as he needed to keep the wire of the fence and the biggest thorns on the most prominent stems between him and the fox.

The fox's breath was foul, and its teeth and eyes stared at him close up. Manny was terrified, but he held his ground, even as fear held time and seemed unwilling to let it pass. At last, the fox turned away. The first two times, she doubled back to see if Manny would fall for the fake. He did not.

When the fox was well out of sight, sound, and smell, Manny ran along the fence-line to the woodpile. He was home. Dropping down through the last knothole that put him where the trails among the rotted wood led to his family's nest, Manny could smell fresh grass. It meant that someone was missing, someone had not returned. The fresh grass was to guide the soul of a disappeared loved one to its nest. He found his mother sitting alone. "What's happened mother?"

"Oh, Manny, it's you," said his mother, bursting into tears and hugging him. "I was afraid I would never see you again. We started quiet time for you."

"A cat flipped me into the warren of a rabbit named Rachel," he began as he raced through the telling of his adventure. "I ran fast and I knew what to do."

"Oh, Manny, I'm so happy. Let me look at you. How did you get that wound in your side?"

"That's where the cat's claw hooked me. Rachel treated it with a paste she makes. It hardly hurts at all unless I think about it."

"Your father, brothers and sisters will be home soon. I can't wait to see their surprise."

Alvin was the first to arrive. "Hey! Manny's here!"

"We thought something had eaten you for sure," said George.

Manny's siblings threw themselves in a heap on top of him as they came into the nest, yelling that they were glad to see him.

"Father's right behind us," said Shyleen.

Fred looked tired. "Speed and endurance, that's what saved me today," he said, flopping down on the wool beside Martha. "Manny? I didn't see you. Where have you been? We thought…well, you know…. It's wonderful. It's wonderful you made it home. We'll sleep well. Everyone made it home safely." He grabbed Manny and hugged him hard and long as he hid his face.

* * *

As Manny fell asleep, his thoughts drifted to Rachel, Farmer Frank, Rusty, Dal, and the scarecrow on the fence-post. He felt himself running, running, running, as he drifted into dream-sleep. He ran faster and faster until he rose into the sky as Zeus and surveyed the land. He hovered above the earth with ballet steps, orchestrating evil to good with pirouettes of his magic rod. It was hard work. Mice were in danger everywhere: to the right, to the left, up ahead, in the rear, close at hand, far away, and everywhere in between.

* * *

Manny awoke with his heart racing. It was the middle of the night. He crawled through the knotholes and passages, emerging at the south end of the woodpile where two boards stuck out about a foot apart, forming a natural porch. Manny would make this porch his haven—a shield from the sun, a shelter from the rain, an amphitheater for the chorus of frogs and crickets.

From Manny's porch, the lands, the creatures, the plants all lay before him. The smells, sounds, and sights were tales of life and death. Here, the heat of day withdrew, the cool of night approached, the sun and moon exchanged domains, the darkness sparkled the stars, the blackness lit the fireflies.

6. Farmer Frank's House

The Franks' house was impossible not to notice. If there was enough light to distinguish the horizon, the house was there. The Franks' farm also had a barn, but it was a motionless form somewhat farther away. The house was alive with movement, lights, and lore.

"There's food in that house," said George one evening when Manny had joined his brothers and sisters to look for seeds. "And it's easy to find, too."

"Who told you that?" asked Bouqueet.

"I overheard Dad and Moses talking about it. Everyone went to the house when the fields were covered with snow. No one could find enough to eat."

"Yeah," said Alvin, "I heard them too. If we didn't have to hunt for food, we'd have more time for fun. Let's check it out."

"Mother told me house food isn't good for us," said Shyleen.

"I know something about the house," said Manny, wishing he had kept his mouth shut.

"You do?!" everyone said almost at the same time.

"Have you been inside?" asked George, anxious that his little brother might have surpassed him in something.

"No, but when I went to Farmer Frank's garden with Rachel, we were close to it, and we met Farmer Frank's new dog, Dal, too," Manny said, although he knew that "met" was not exactly what had happened.

Alvin was jealous. "If you haven't been inside, I intend to be the first one."

"Nobody's going without me," said George. "You can't know too much about where to find something to eat."

"Mother will never let us go," said Shyleen.

"So, who's going to ask?" said George. "And if you tell, we'll never take you with us again—no matter where we go. You'll be on your own."

"Let's all go," said Caressa. "I'd like to feel what it's like to walk on the floor of a house. Do you think it's just like a field? I want to touch everything in the house."

"I'd like to smell what's in there," said Bouqueet. "People must smell really different from animals. And their food, too." She sniffed the air long and deep, as though she might smell something even from where they were.

"I don't know," said Shyleen. "Let's just stay home and let George and Alvin go. They can tell us what they find."

"They'd say anything just to make us jealous," said Caressa. "They might not go in the house at all, but say they did."

"We need to leave now," said Manny—as though announcing a decision he had made long before. "Otherwise, we won't get back before morning."

And just like that, Manny had taken charge. Even though he had not actually been to the house, it seemed perfectly natural to lead them across the pasture, as though it was something he did every day. He was not afraid. He was Zeus.

A starless sky wrapped them in darkness on their journey to the house. Yet, the broad outlines of the garden fence, the barn, and the house remained visible even after the lights in the house went out, closing its eyes for the night.

Manny led his band of uninvited guests on a route that took them just beyond the north end of the garden, opposite the end where he had entered it with Rachel. He looked down the fence-line for the scarecrow. She was there. She didn't care if he came to the garden or to the house. She was inviting him to share her fresh carrots, lettuce, and peas. It was food for a field mouse.

"What are you looking at?" whispered Bouqueet.

"Nothing," he lied, knowing it didn't sound convincing.

As they passed the end of the garden nearest the house where the second scarecrow was, Manny looked up at it, hoping to see the same smile, the same invitation. But this scarecrow was not smiling. It returned Manny's look, disapproving, with a deeply furrowed brow, its face the mask of President Abraham Lincoln. Farmer Frank had worn the mask to the same Halloween party as Mrs. Frank had worn her mask of Marilyn Monroe, the blond movie star.

Although deeply lined, the face was not angry or threatening. It was a worried, fatherly face that said, "Now you look here, young fella. You know this is not your daddy's garden. Before you go gettin' into any trouble here, you just think it over and do what's right." With no movement in the air, the scarecrow's torn, dark suit hung loose, its bearer, sad, burdened with choices.

Manny wanted to assure this austere figure that he had not come back to enter the garden. He wanted the scarecrow to give him a sign that it was all right to be there. But President Lincoln did not smile, did not nod, did not move in the breezeless night air.

"Hurry," said Shyleen, who was the last one to pass him. "I don't trust Alvin taking the lead."

"I heard Dad say they got in the house through a crack in the foundation," yelled Alvin. "I think I see it."

They squeezed through the crack in the foundation and found themselves in a large cavern with a dirt floor. Near where they entered, a pipe came down through an opening in the floor above them and disappeared into the earth. They were right below the kitchen sink. One by one, they climbed up the pipe and huddled together in the dark, small space of the cabinet under the kitchen sink where they found themselves. No one said anything. What to do now?

The closed-in space held them in its hand, threatening to clench them should they move. Manny scanned for any crack of light, seeking an exit.

Bouqueet was held by the profusion of unfamiliar smells. She also smelled mice, though their smell was not quite the same as she was used to.

George knew that some of the smells meant food, but what kind?

Caressa put her feet down carefully on the unfamiliar floor, testing how it felt, testing if it was safe to walk upon.

Alvin wanted to say something funny to break the tension, but he was too scared.

Shyleen wished she'd stayed at home with her mother.

"Hello," said a voice from behind a large container next to them. "Welcome to our home. My name is Maggie, and this is my sister Winnie and our brother..."

"Marvelous Maxwell Mouse, is my name," interrupted her brother. "Actually, that's my stage name. It's a little long, so I tell everyone to call me Triple M. I do tricks to entertain everyone."

"His name is Mud," said Maggie, "and no one has ever called him Marvelous Maxwell Mouse, or Triple M, for that matter."

"But they will this winter. I have a trick I'm working on that will knock 'em dead with laughter."

"My name's Manny, and these are my brothers, George and Alvin, and my sisters, Shyleen, Caressa, and Bouqueet. We live in the woodpile down the fence-line. Do you live here?"

"Yes, this is where we were born. Our parents disappeared here. So, we stayed behind when the other mice left for the fields."

"It's a great life," interrupted Mud with an air of importance and his eyes cast at Bouqueet. "There's plenty of food, and lots of mice will come back when the snow falls again. We'll drive the cat crazy."

"Is the cat's name Flora?" asked Manny.

"Yes, how did you know?" answered Maggie.

"I sort of met her in the fields. She probably killed one of our neighbors."

"I'm sorry to hear that. She does get lucky sometimes— or a mouse gets careless. It's best to play it safe, Mother always said."

"You can't have any fun playing it safe," said Mud. "Anyway, I'm much more clever than Flora. I'm famous for my tricks on her, on the dogs, and on Mr. and Mrs. Frank too. What do you think of this? I wait inside the cabinet by the glassware. First thing in the morning, when Mrs. Frank comes into the kitchen and opens the cabinet door, I'm standing on my hind legs, staring right at her, with my teeth bared. She'll faint for sure. I know the other mice will be chanting 'Triple M, Triple M' when they see *that* trick."

"In your dreams," said Winnie rolling her eyes. "You've been more lucky than clever so far."

"It's not luck. It's planning. You'll see."

"Is there any food in this house?" asked George, directing his question and attention to Maggie.

"George, don't be rude," said Bouqueet. "We're not beggars. We have plenty to eat in the fields."

"It's all right," said Maggie. "Lots of mice come into the house for the food. It's why our parents made their nest in here, they said."

"No offence," said Bouqueet, "but the food doesn't smell very good."

"Oh, that's the food the Franks put in that container there. We're used to it. We don't eat that. Mud, show them to the food pantry."

"Wait," said Bouqueet, "There's one delicious smell here too."

"Oh, that's the cheese in the trap. I almost forgot that's why we came in here," said Winnie.

"Yeah, wait 'til you taste the cheese," said Mud.

"What's a trap?" asked Manny.

"A trap," said Mud, "is a device Mrs. Frank puts in here hoping to kill us. Someday, I plan to organize a gang to move the trap to the middle of the kitchen and set it off in the morning just as Mrs. Frank enters the kitchen door. She'll jump to the ceiling when that thing snaps where she's not expecting it. They'll be talking about Marvelous Maxwell Mouse for generations when I pull that off."

"And while you're laughing over how clever you are, Mrs. Frank will be taking the broom to your head," said Winnie. "The trap is behind this pail where the bad smells come from. I think Mrs. Frank thinks it's the bad smells that bring us in here, so this is where she puts the trap."

The trap was a small wood platform with some metal parts and a cube of cheese resting on a raised piece of metal in its center.

"The way the trap works," explained Maggie, "is that if you move the metal piece holding the cheese, that bar lying on the other side flips over and comes smashing down to pin you under it. If you don't die from the blow, you're caught until Mrs. Frank comes to get you."

"The trap only works," said Mud, stepping to the center of the trap in front of the cheese, "if you try to eat the cheese where it's resting in the trap. You have to lift the cheese off the metal piece that holds it. I learned by watching a field mouse get smashed trying."

Mud lifted the cheese from the trigger. "Voila!" he said balancing the cheese on one paw in a showy manner only to have the cheese fall off his paw. Maggie and Winnie inhaled a quick breath, but the cheese fell harmlessly to the side of the trigger. The spring remained taut. The deadly steel bar remained open. Instead of the sound of steel on mouse, there was only the anxious breathing of nine mice.

"That was lucky," said Winnie.

"It wasn't luck," lied Mud. But he was shaking and steadied himself by grabbing onto the cheese and quickly rolling it out of the trap. "How about a cheer for Marvelous Maxwell Mouse?"

Everyone ignored him. "This tastes great," said Winnie. "Much better than the cheese Mrs. Frank usually puts in the trap. Maybe she thought we'd get so excited, we'd make a mistake."

"Well, it almost worked," said Manny, as he took a taste.

"The best part is yet to come," said Mud. "Follow me to the pantry. You won't believe all the good stuff to eat in there."

One of the doors to the kitchen sink cabinet was slightly warped, leaving a space for them to slip out into the kitchen.

"To tell the truth," said Bouqueet, "I'm feeling nauseated from all the strange smells. I don't know if I can eat anything."

"After a few days in the house, it'll smell normal," said Mud.

Bouqueet knew she'd never get used to it. "What about Flora and the dogs, and Farmer and Mrs. Frank? Don't they mind if we're eating everything?"

"Well, I guess that's why Mrs. Frank puts out the trap," said Maggie. "But they're sound asleep. Rusty's gotten old. His nose is gone. He doesn't hear well. Old Farmer Frank is the same way. The cat's no young chick either. Once in bed, she's out for the night, and the new dog sleeps outside."

Caressa was fascinated by the feel of the linoleum on the kitchen floor. It was cool and perfectly smooth to the touch, and it felt like you could slide on it and roll around on it without getting your hair dirty.

"Come into the pantry," urged Mud. "Chew into any box you find, and you're almost certain to find something delicious."

Shyleen went straight for the bag of rice. Caressa was eating Cheerios. "These little black fruit things are sweet," said Alvin, holding up a raisin.

Manny did not like what was happening. What if Flora showed up? "Let's go," he said. "We've had enough to eat."

"I don't know if I ever want to leave," said George. "Just look at all this food! And you don't have to walk to find it."

"The best is yet to come. Follow me to the chocolate bowl," said Mud, running for another room.

George cast an eye back to Maggie. "Is this a trick?"

"Mud loves to play tricks, but this is for real. Chocolate really tastes good. Mud! Don't take more than one. We'll all share. We don't want Farmer and Mrs. Frank to notice some is gone."

Mud and George ran ahead and everyone but Caressa followed. She stayed behind, ran one direction and slid before rolling onto her side. She couldn't believe how different this floor was from anything else she had ever stepped on.

In the living room, Mud climbed onto the couch and onto a small table next to it where there was a glass dish filled with chocolate stars. He pulled one out of the dish and pushed it off the table. Everyone took a turn to get a bite.

"Hurry up, Caressa," yelled Bouqueet. "I'll save you a piece, but if you're too slow, I might eat it. It's really delicious."

"I'm coming," Caressa said, but she slowed as soon as she entered the living room, where the center of the floor was covered by a Turkish carpet. Caressa felt the wool. It was soft and warm, like the wool of their nest, only different. It felt like it was suspending her just slightly off the ground. She walked next to Bouqueet and accepted the small piece of chocolate Bouqueet had saved for her. She held it briefly and felt how it immediately softened, responding to the warmth of her paws. "Nothing I've ever held before felt like this," she said.

"Better yet, nothing I've ever tasted has been close to this sweet," said George.

"It's time for us to get back to the woodpile," said Manny. The air in the house was eerily unmoving. Outdoors, air could carry the smell of danger, but here, the smell of danger did not approach from any particular direction but hovered oppressively from all sides.

"What's the hurry?" asked George. "Maggie, do you want us to leave?"

"You're welcome to stay as long as you wish, but if your parents are waiting, you shouldn't make them think you disappeared. You can always come back. We'll be happy to see you again."

In the end, George agreed to leave, saying he'd be back. And, indeed, secretly, each of them knew they would come back. The house was a store of riches, waiting to be discovered, a vault of adventures, waiting to be experienced.

7. Gophericious

Manny awoke toward dusk and climbed up through the paths in the rotted wood and out onto his porch. The darkening sky tumbled clouds from the west, and the smell of rain fell on the soil and plants, promising moisture, promising life. Manny loved cloudy days. The extra humidity accentuated every smell. He ran west into the cornfield to meet the clouds and waited out the rain under the leaves of a hog weed, listening to the music of the rain on the earth until it softened and ceased.

The silence that followed was short, broken by the splash, splash, splash, splash, splash of large animal footsteps. They were fleet footsteps, fox footsteps, but not coming his direction. With the strong smells left by the rain, Manny doubted the fox would smell him, but he hid in a clump of fragrant onion grass.

Suddenly, the fox's footsteps shifted, running directly toward him and preceded by the sound of flurried smaller feet spitting through the puddles—pit, pit, pit, pit, pit. Coming toward him as fast as its legs could carry him was a gopher with pretty dark stripes on its brown body. Manny knew it would be running for safety, running for its hole. He bolted forward in a straight line opposite from where they were coming and spied the gopher's hole just as fear vacuumed the air from his lungs.

"Into the hole!" yelled the gopher, slamming Manny from behind, knocking him tail to head down into the depths, and scrambling over him to lead the way down. "That fox is no slouch in the digging department. Stay beside me. I'll be digging for our lives."

Manny did not need urging. The gopher was quick, but in the tunnel down, Manny was a match for him. They reached the bottom in seconds. The gopher set about digging with furry, dirt flying out behind them. The fox was digging too. Long, strong strokes: fump, fump, fump.

Still, Manny sensed no fear in the gopher. His legs scratched much faster than the fox's: chi, chi, chi, chi, chi. After a short while, the gopher turned and started to dig upward and then in a new direction. At last, he stopped, and they sat listening to the heavy scratching of the fox's strong legs. The scratching lightened and then stopped. The fox was listening and smelling, catching her breath. Fump, fump, fump resumed the noise, although it seemed to Manny there was less heart in it. The fox stopped again. She waited—but not long. Hunger turned her nose to the wind and another promise of dinner.

Manny and his new friend, the gopher, stayed still for a long time. Then, without speaking, the gopher began to dig. He dug back toward where the fox had excavated a large hole. When he got there, he dug straight down again, made a couple of turns, and hollowed out an area big enough for a nest.

"The opening at the top will smell strong of fox. Good protection. I recommend you stay here tonight. My name's Go, by the way. Well, my real name is Gophericious, Godominic, Gopherberg, Gopherian, Gophersky, Gopherov, Gopherson. You see, I was named after my maternal grandfather, Gophericious. Godominic is my patron saint, and the rest of the names trace our lineage back to when there were dinosaurs right here in this field. Anyway, people just call me Go, because it's easier, and I don't mind. Also, I'm on the go a lot, being a gopher, if you know what I mean. Go, go, go. That's pretty much all I do, but it has its moments. What's your name, little feller?"

"Manny. Just Manny. It's my name, and it's what everyone calls me. I live in the woodpile toward where the sun comes up. Have you ever been there?"

"Of course, I know the place. I pretty much know every landmark around here, being on the go as I am. Looks like you do a fair amount of running too. Strongest lookin' legs I've ever seen on a mouse."

"Thank you. I'm building up my legs for when running can save my life."

"Personally, I never thought about running to build up my legs. It's just what I was born to do. I run. I go. I scamper. I dash. Sometimes I see animals—cows for instance—just idly grazing as though they have their whole lifetimes to get their eating done. I'm not made that way. I have to grab my food, wolf it down, and get back on the road."

"Gopher-r-i-sc-i-i?" stammered Manny, embarrassed as he realized he'd got the name wrong.

"It's Gophericious, son, but don't worry about it. Really, just call me Go. I don't mind. Anyway, I think of Go as a metaphor for my life. Poetic in that sense, don't you think?"

Manny thought Go was really a most unpoetic name, but he wasn't about to say that. "Oh, yes, now that you mention it," Manny lied, "Go *is* a poetic metaphor."

Gophericious heard the skepticism in Manny's voice. "Well, enough of that," he said to break the awkward silence. "We need to rest. We'll be on the go tomorrow—at least I will." He let out a long, deep breath, and Manny watched him fall asleep instantly.

Manny lay thinking. Tomorrow, he would work on survival training. Tonight, he wanted to indulge in fantasy, in magic, to dream of Zeus, a mouse faster, stronger, wiser than any creature on earth—and maybe a good poet, as well.

* * *

In Manny's dream, a fox chased Gophericious straight toward where Zeus was sitting down to eat. Not only did Zeus not like to see foxes chasing innocent gophers with the intent to eat them, he particularly did not like having his dinner interrupted. He slowly raised his head, completed chewing the food in his mouth, and stood up just as Gophericious sped by.

The fox, shocked to see this mouse with the jagged white mark on his chest and rod in his paw seemingly offering himself up for dinner, jerked his head toward the mouse in full stride, thinking to snap it up for an appetizer and continue on after the gopher, which would be the main course.

But instead of a morsel of mouse, the fox found his mouth plowed into the earth in one motion and his hind feet leaving the ground in another. Zeus had jammed the fox's head into the soil while its mouth was open and then ducked under the fox's belly, lifting it high into the air. Zeus flew round and round in a tight circle, making the fox dizzy and nauseous.

"Please put me down," pleaded the fox, spitting dirt. "I think I'm going to throw up. Who are you, anyway?"

Zeus did not answer. He just turned faster and faster around in a tight circle until the fox emptied his stomach. The fox looked green. "Oh, please put me down. What have I done to you? Oh, oh, I think I'm going to die. Please put me down. Aagh." He vomited a second time.

Zeus deposited the fox high up in a large tree where the trunk split into three branches, forming the kind of juncture that is perfect for building a tree-house. But foxes don't have proper claws for holding onto a tree—not even an easy perch with three branches. Consequently, foxes can't climb trees, and they are afraid of heights.

The fox was trying not to look down. "Please carry me back down. The tree is moving, my stomach is in my brain, and my legs are shaking."

Zeus sat on a branch nearby, thinking about what the appropriate punishment should be. "I could just leave you here," he said at last. "You might die of starvation. No, actually, you would die of thirst, I think. On the other hand, you might get attacked by vultures and be eaten slowly, bite by bite."

The fox's eyes opened wider and wider. He looked up to see if there were any vultures hovering.

"Your mostly likely fate," continued Zeus, "will be to lose your grip and simply fall out of the tree. On the way down, you might have a nice view. Try to enjoy it, because the landing will hurt."

The fox shifted his weight trying to get more secure in the cradle of the three branches, but instead, he almost fell.

"My advice," said Zeus, "is that you not move. I'm going back down to finish my dinner."

"Please don't leave me. If you take me down with you, I'll just sit quietly beside you while you have your dinner."

"Just don't move, and you'll be okay. And try not to look down. I don't want you to fall while I'm eating. That would be a mess."

* * *

Manny awoke hungry.

"Good, you're awake," said Gophericious. "I hope you don't mind, but I've really got to get going."

"Not at all Mr. Go," said Manny feeling he should have used Gophericious' real name but afraid he might mispronounce it. "I need to get home. My parents will be worried. I didn't thank you for saving my life."

"Oh, that was nothing. It was my fault you were in danger anyway."

"If you get by the woodpile sometime, come see us."

"Thank you. I might just do that. I do get by there every now and again. I get pretty much everywhere being on the go as I am. Well, take care. I'm off."

Manny watched Gophericious run in the general direction that he would be going, but he knew he could not keep up. Anyway, he didn't feel like running fast at this moment. He was hungry and set out to find corn.

8. Caressa's Quest

Farmer Frank's house was on all the children's minds, but no one said anything. George could not forget the chocolate. He was definitely going back.

Caressa was thinking that when she made her own nest, she wanted something special to line it with—maybe a material even softer and warmer than wool. What she knew was that this material, whatever it was, would be found in Farmer and Mrs. Frank's house, and she was going back to find it.

Alvin thought Mud had the right idea. A mouse should live where there was time and opportunity for fun. Working together, their potential was unlimited.

Shyleen's head told her to stay at home, and she wanted to. But if everyone else went, she would go too.

Although the smells had made her nauseous, Bouqueet rationalized a return for educational purposes. Who knew when recognizing scents unique to the inside of a house might save one from danger?

Manny lay awake for a long time. He did not even consider whether they would return. He knew it was inevitable, but he wanted to go alone. He eased himself away from everyone and started up the path through the rotted wood, climbing through the knothole that led to the broad corridor of the hollow tree-trunk.

"Wait for me." It was Caressa. "I want to go back to the house to find a cloth for my nest. Will you go with me?"

"Yes, I'll go with you." It was not what Manny had intended, but since he was not clear on why he was returning to the house, helping Caressa presented him with a purpose for it. Maybe this visit would end it for him—he'd feel no need to return ever again. That would be accomplishment enough.

"Wait for us. We're going too. You didn't think you could have the chocolate all to yourselves, did you?" It was George with Alvin, Shyleen, and Bouqueet.

"Yeah, Caressa," said Shyleen. "What's so special you can't share with us? Mice share everything. It's what Mom and Dad taught us about survival."

"I'm not going for food. I want to find something special to make a nest with, like ours, only maybe just a little different, that's all. I intended to share it."

"I can sleep on a rock if my stomach is full," said George. "Who cares what else is in the house. The food's the prize."

"Everybody can do what they want when we get there," said Shyleen. "There's no point in arguing about it."

"Especially not now," said Manny. "We need to hurry so we can get back to the woodpile before the sun comes up. Let's go."

Manny took the lead, running fast enough to keep everybody moving and slowing when he saw anyone falling behind. They went north toward the house, following the fence, which was overgrown with weeds, bushes, and vines and defined by a line of trees: dogwood, pear, sassafras, and mulberry. At the base of the mulberry tree, Manny turned east into the open pasture and toward the house.

Manny glanced at the scarecrows. They were not moving and seemed not to disapprove. He ran into the tall grass and weeds of the pasture, yelling, "Run! Your life depends on it."

Everyone made it through the crack in the foundation and on up to the cabinet under the kitchen sink. Manny, Shyleen, and Bouqueet agreed to help Caressa search for cloth, while George and Alvin chose to go to the pantry.

In the living room, Manny spotted Maggie and Winnie coming out from under the couch. "Hello," he called. "You're Maggie and Winnie, right?"

"Yes, we were hoping you'd come back. Would you like some chocolate?" asked Winnie.

"Not now. Caressa wants to look for material she could use to build a nest."

"Yes, something soft and warm, like wool, only maybe different," said Caressa. "I don't mean wool isn't good. It's wonderful. My mother made *her* nest with wool. I just want something different, that's all."

"Try that blouse lying on the couch. It's silk," said Winnie.

Caressa climbed onto the couch. She walked on the blouse. She lay down on it. She rolled over on it. "Wow, this is completely different, different from wool, from grass, from leaves, from the rug, from the couch, from the kitchen floor, from anything else I've ever touched. My feet don't sink into it. They glide across it. And it's warm, too. I have to have this material for my nest."

"That's much too big to take with us," said Bouqueet.

"There are many different types and sizes of material in the room where Farmer and Mrs. Frank sleep," said Maggie, pointing to the open door off the living room. "But we don't go in there, because Rusty and Flora sleep in there, too."

"I'm going in anyway," announced Caressa. "Everyone's asleep, right? I'll just look around a little."

"I don't think it's safe," Shyleen said.

"No one will hear me," insisted Caressa. "I'm a mouse." And with that, she ran through the open bedroom door.

"Let's wait here," said Manny, stopping at the entrance to the bedroom. "We'll be able to see if Rusty or Flora stirs in time to warn her."

In the bedroom, Caressa went crazy, dancing on every piece of clothing she could find, rubbing her face and feet in each piece to get its full effect. Rolling and snuggling into some. She swung from clothing draped over chairs. She scampered up clothing hanging in the closet. She burrowed into clothes in the clothes basket.

Unfortunately, nothing was exactly right. Most of what she found was too large to be easily moved. Some pieces were small but did not have any special feel. There were wool socks in the clothes basket, but they smelled bad, and, anyway, wool was not what she wanted.

She had about given up when she saw a small piece of cloth draped off the top of the nightstand beside the bed next to where Mrs. Frank was sleeping. It had the sheen of silk and the allure of being that last and surely lucky chance to find exactly what she was looking for.

Caressa went to the far side of the bed and climbed up to the second shelf of books on a bookcase next to the nightstand. From there, she could just about reach the cloth, which she was sure had to be silk. She leaped off the book nearest to the cloth and grabbed onto it with her claws. Briefly, she was hanging, dangling mid-air, half-way up the nightstand. She reached out with one front paw to pull herself up, except the cloth began to slide toward her ever so slowly, forcing her to dig in where she was, holding onto the cloth, holding in her breath, and holding to the hope that she could steal this prize and make it hers.

The cloth slid slowly at first. Caressa knew that if she let go of it, she could drop back down to the floor effortlessly and silently. But she could not. She was holding onto desire, onto hope, onto a dream to have a nest unlike any other. It was such a small thing to ask—just a little piece of cloth from this vast treasure of textiles, a piece surely too small and of too little value to be missed by the keeper of this treasury. She could not let go.

The cloth continued to lower her toward the floor until the empty glass resting on it reached the edge of the nightstand. Caressa looked up just as the glass was tilting toward her. It was too late. She and the glass crashed to the floor with the cloth tumbling over and around her and the glass shattering in several pieces. It missed Caressa directly, but she was cut by a shard as she struggled to get untangled from the silk.

Flora leaped off the bed. Rusty gave a puzzled woof. Farmer Frank sat up. And Mrs. Frank pulled the light chain.

9. The Tale of George's Tail

Manny could not see Caressa, but he knew she needed time to find a hiding place. If he could draw the Franks' attention away.... "Follow me," he yelled as he ran toward the kitchen where Mud, George, and Alvin had heard the noise.

"What happened?" asked George.

"I'll explain later," said Manny. "Everyone into the cabinet. Mud, set off the trap."

"Let me do it," said George, looking at Maggie for her approval and attention.

"Mud, set off the trap," repeated Manny.

George was annoyed, and to show he could have done it, he gave directions: "Crowd in close to the trigger and push down so the trap arm comes over your head and smashes down without hitting you."

Mud was careful, curling his tail in tight around him, positioning himself well inside of where the spring-loaded arm would land. He pushed on the cheese. SMASH!! They knew the sound was coming, yet they jumped when it happened.

George jumped the highest. He had not been as careful as Mud. In a nervous, anticipatory twitch as the arm came down, George's tail flicked under its path. He was caught.

"Ow, ow, ow, aaahh, my tail is caught," yelled George, jumping around with the trap attached to the end of his tail. "My tail is killing me. Get this thing off me. It hurts something terrible. Please, please, uu, ow, aaahhh!!"

"Everyone jump on the trap, so it can't move," yelled Manny. "George, pull as hard as you can; pull until your tail breaks off, if you have to."

"Ow, aaah. It hurts too much when I pull. Ow, aah."

Manny smelled Flora in the kitchen a second later. She had her paw under the edge of the door and was pulling on it. It snapped back shut, but Mrs. Frank's hand caught it. She had a broom in her hand, and in a flash, all the mice, except Manny and George, slipped around behind the drainpipe and under the floor.

Manny hid behind the garbage pail to see what would happen. George was completely exposed. Manny could see George's little heart pounding so hard it seemed ready to jump out of his chest. His was pumping too. Flora appeared just behind Mrs. Frank.

"What's going on?" yelled Farmer Frank from somewhere in the kitchen. Rusty barked but not with much enthusiasm. Flora seemed about to enter the cabinet when the door slammed shut.

"The trap has a mouse by its tail," said Mrs. Frank. I'll sweep the trap out with the broom. Then you grab the mouse if Flora doesn't."

Manny watched the door open again. This time Mrs. Frank stuck the broom inside the cabinet and swept George and the trap up against the cabinet wall. George groaned and bravely tried to run away with the trap on his tail, only Mrs. Frank swept him and the trap up against the wall again. George groaned even louder and fell still, lying on his side, anticipating the next blow. He didn't realize the tip of his tail had broken off. He was free.

"Run for the pipe!" shouted Manny, "Your tail broke off. Quick!"

George righted himself just as the broom came at him again and swept him out of the cabinet. He landed on his feet and was running, though not very fast, as he disappeared from Manny's view. The whole thing took Flora by surprise, so that it seemed to Manny that George could possibly have reached a nearby hiding spot. The cabinet door opened again, and Manny slipped behind the pipe and down under the floor before Mrs. Frank could hit him with the broom.

In the crawl space under the kitchen, Manny, Alvin, Mud, Bouqueet, Shyleen, Winnie, and Maggie were huddled together, waiting, their eyes wide and turned to the floor above them, their hearts a beat too fast, and their bodies still in the excitement of fear.

"Your plan worked," said Bouqueet after awhile. "Everybody came out of the bedroom when the trap went off. Maybe Caressa escaped."

"Let's go find her," said Shyleen.

"Not now," said Manny. "She knows to keep hidden. So does George. We'll come back, but right now, we need to go home. We don't want our parents to think we *all* disappeared."

"Just great," said Alvin with a tone of self-pity. "They get to stay here and eat chocolate, and we have to go home and tell Mom and Dad that we came to Farmer Frank's and who knows what's happened to George and Caressa. How about I stay here and eat chocolate? You don't need me."

"Yes we do. I'm not going to tell Mother you preferred chocolate to coming home."

"I don't know how George could have escaped," said Bouqueet. "Probably Flora ate him." As soon as she said it, she felt terrible.

"I doubt it; Flora's well fed," said Manny trying to be optimistic but knowing that George stood no better chance of survival as Flora's toy than as her dinner.

10. Waiting for the Disappeared

It was a slow, silent trip back. No one was eager to return. No one wanted to talk about what had to be spoken. Approaching the woodpile, Bouqueet finally raised the subject on all of their minds, "What will we say to mother?"

"We could say we don't know what happened to them," said Alvin. "We don't actually know, do we?"

"We shouldn't have gone to the house," said Shyleen.

"Going to the house wasn't the problem," said Alvin. "George and Caressa got careless. If you're careless, you can get eaten in the fields just as easily."

"Don't talk about getting eaten, Alvin," said Bouqueet. "That's so gross. They're probably just hiding. We can say they stayed behind, because they like it there. That's not a lie. George does like it—at least he likes the food—and he told me he liked Maggie, too, but I wasn't supposed to tell anyone about that."

"Caressa wanted to be at the house, too," said Shyleen, "at least long enough to find a special kind of material for a nest."

Manny said nothing. They entered the woodpile and followed the paths that led deep among the rotted wood to their nest, where the earth kept it warm in winter and cool in summer. It had never felt so good to be there.

Their mother was waiting and hugged each of them in turn. Manny was the last. "Mother, George and Caressa got separated from us. We don't know what happened to them."

"Where were you?" asked their mother, her face anxious, her eyes moist.

"In Farmer Frank's house. There was a noise, and Mrs. Frank and the cat came after us. Caressa and George got separated from us. They're probably hiding. The house has many good hiding places."

"I know."

"You do?" asked Shyleen. "Have you been to the house?"

"Yes, all of us in the woodpile went last winter," she began as her memories brought images of many places in the house where a mouse could hide, could be safe, and she visualized her children in one of them, waiting for her to come and find them. "The snow covered the fields a long time. We couldn't find enough to eat. Come, let's huddle together and be silent for George and Caressa. They need our spiritual connection with them."

They rested, pressed together, each with his own thoughts, until all were asleep in the warmth of the wool and the protection of the woodpile along the fence between the pasture and the corn field on Farmer Frank's farm.

Manny heard his parents whisper, and he felt them leave the nest. He waited briefly, then, followed from a distance. He could hear them talking.

"I think I should go alone," said Fred. "If we both go, the children will know. We can't ask them not to go, if they see us going."

"I have to go. Even if George and Caressa have found each other, they may be afraid to leave. They'll be waiting for us to come."

"What will we tell the children when they ask where we've been?"

"The truth. We've raised fine children. They're ready to make their own lives, and we will accept the choices they make. I'm not staying behind."

Martha started north up the fence-line, and Fred hurried to catch up. Manny followed them. The dark had no relief. No single star shone. The temperature was dropping too fast for the season, and a damp wind announced the cold front sliding down the east side of the Blue Ridge foothills. Within minutes, a cold, driving rain sent Manny back to the woodpile and down to the nest. His fur was wet, and it felt good to nestle in against his siblings, who were sound asleep. Minutes later, his parents returned. It was not a night to be out.

The next morning, the sun was high when Manny left the nest and started up the path that led to his porch. If the weather held, he knew his parents would go to Farmer

Frank's that night. He was undecided if he would follow. "Manny, wait for me," said a small voice. It was Bouqueet. "I want to go with you. I'm afraid to be on my own, today."

Manny wished he felt confident about being safe. He knew he was not Zeus, not the Lord of Lightning, not the Titan of Thunder. Much as he wished, he could not do the magical things he fantasized. "Okay," he said, "we can look for food together. You can teach me new smells."

"That will be easy. Interesting smells are everywhere, even here in the woodpile. The wood of each type of tree smells unique: pine, oak, persimmon, apple, walnut, maple, mulberry, cherry, sassafras, ash—they're all in this woodpile."

Once outside, they headed south down the fence-line, and Bouqueet pointed out the special smells of several weeds: spiderwort, sneezeweed, goldenrod, milkweed. In between, they ate corn and seeds.

"Now let's run for awhile," Manny said at last. "Speed and endurance. You never know when it can save you."

They ran and rested and ran some more. "No wonder your leg muscles are so powerful," said Bouqueet after awhile. "Have you been doing this every day? I'm exhausted, and you look like you're just getting warmed up."

"Well, actually, when I'm alone, I run longer. If you come out with me for a few more days, you'll run because your legs want to, and a rhythm in your mind sets the pace, like music. It's a fantastic feeling."

The sun was above them when they found the newly forming sour cherries on a tree south of the woodpile next to the oaks. They ate until they were full, and Manny began to feel sleepy. "I need a nap. A place where we can sleep without worrying about a predator."

"I smell honeysuckle in that direction." Bouqueet pointed south.

"Are you sure? I don't smell anything."

"I have the best nose, remember? While you've been running, I've been training to survive too, you know. Follow me."

Manny caught the scent minutes later. The honeysuckle was about to bloom and growing densely over and around the fence.

"No animal will smell us in there," said Bouqueet.

Manny looked into the honeysuckle growth and saw a pile of the previous fall's leaves stuck at the base, forming a comfortable place to take a nap. He slept deeply.

* * *

In Manny's dream, Zeus was watching a mouse family escape from a wild cat by running along a thin branch lying across a creek. The mice were about half-way across the creek, and the cat was testing the branch with her front paws. But it bent under her weight and was not big enough for her claws to get a grip. The cat looked at the water. It was not particularly deep, but cats don't like to get wet. The cat hesitated and looked to see if there was another way across the creek.

The mice would have been safely to the other side, except that the last one turned back to see if the cat was coming after them. He slipped. Only the swift reaction of Zeus, his nostrils filling with the smell of water and moss as he swooped in low, saved the little creature an inch from the creek's thirst.

* * *

Manny jerked awake, sensing an unusual smell, and found himself looking straight into the mesmerizing stare of a large blacksnake. The snake was looking at him through an opening among the drooping leaves. It thrust its forked tongue toward Manny repeatedly, but his head hardly moved. Its eyes were glued open and on Manny.

Manny knew what he had to do. He had to move. He had to break the line of sight. But he was a block of ice, frozen in place. He could hear Bouqueet breathing beside him still asleep. If she moved, the snake might divert its gaze. Even the slightest change in the snake's stare would free him. He trembled. His powerful legs tensed, ready to spring him to freedom. But he could not give them the order to move. His brain would not send instructions. It was immobile, like the rest of him.

The snake inched forward, flicking its tongue as it arched forward without adjusting its stare. It was in no hurry. And Manny also watched, no, stared right back, unable to do anything else. He watched death approach with outward peace and inward terror.

The snake arched its front third forward as its rear two-thirds slithered slowly toward Manny, who could not make himself so much as blink, though he knew that was all it would take. If the slightest breeze moved one leaf, if Manny could muster one blink, one nod of the head, one kick of a foot or shrug of a shoulder, he would be free. With all the force of mind he could muster, he tried to make some, any, just one muscle respond to the terror he felt in the cold eyes of the snake with its forked tongue flicking at him.

What responded wasn't a muscle. It was his nose. As he stared at the snake's eyes, the unusual and subtle smell of the snake gave way to a smell that enveloped and overpowered all others. DOGBREATH! Manny still could not make a single muscle in his body respond, but he understood that everything was about to change. As the snake's upper body made another short lurch forward, Dal came crashing into view, snatching the snake in his mouth and whipping it sharply right to left, right to left, right to left, furiously swinging the snake, a low, angry growl scratching from deep in his throat. Grrrrrrrrrrrr…

Bouqueet awakened with a start. "Don't move," Manny whispered. "Farmer Frank's young Dalmatian is about to finish off that snake."

As he spoke, half the snake snapped off and landed a few feet away. Dal dropped the other half and circled around it. Then he walked over to the other half and circled it. The battle was won. Dal turned and proudly loped away.

"Oh my God," whispered Bouqueet. "The dog just snapped the snake in half. Why did he attack the snake? He didn't eat it."

"He doesn't attack for food. He attacks because it moves. He killed it, because he can't take a chance with a snake.

There are copperheads and rattlers out here that could kill him."

"Should we try to thank him?"

"It might not be safe. He's just a young dog, chasing whatever moves."

They walked out to where the snake lay, approaching the rear half of the snake first. It was twisting and turning. The front half, lying a short distance away, also continued writhing in place. There was a strong smell of blood, moisture, and another smell that Bouqueet decided must be death. In spite of her love of smells, she found these disgusting and wanted to get away as quickly as possible. Manny walked toward the front half of the snake.

"What are you doing? Aren't you afraid? What if it puts itself together and comes after us?"

"It can't hurt us now. I want to see it up close. Maybe I'll learn something." Manny watched the front half twist and turn, but it was slowing down. Its eyes were closed, and its mouth was hardly moving any more.

11. A Rescue Plan

"Where have you been?" asked Shyleen when they returned to the woodpile.

"Survival training," said Bouqueet. "We found some delicious cherries. And a snake crept up on us while we took a nap, only a dog came and bit the snake and shook it until it snapped in half. The blood smelled foul, and both halves of the snake were moving as though they were still alive. It was horrible."

"Yeah, well that's why I don't want to spend my life looking for food in the fields," said Alvin. "In Mrs. Frank's kitchen, the food is so easy you have time to enjoy other things."

"Speaking of Farmer Frank's house," said Shyleen, "when are we going back to find George and Caressa?"

"As soon as we get a dry night," said Manny.

But cold spring thundershowers appeared every late afternoon as regular as the sun moved toward the horizon, stopping sometime before dawn. Watching the pattern, Manny developed a plan. He would go up the fence-line during the day and find cover from the rain near Farmer Frank's house. When the rain stopped, he'd be able to reach the house before the sun came up.

From his porch the next day, Manny watched steam rise from the grass, which hung heavy with water from the previous night's rain. The resulting fog lay just above the grass, looking as though it might be the previous night's clouds, which, having emptied of water, had settled onto the earth—tired and not eager to rise. But the sun was calling the moisture, the vapor was rising, the clouds were gathering, and the cycle for another night's rain was well underway.

Manny waited most of the day before starting up the fence-line toward Farmer Frank's. Not all the moisture was gone from the grass. He traveled tight in among the weeds and vines growing along and over the fence to keep dry and protected.

"Wait for us," said a voice Manny recognized as Shyleen's.

"Why didn't you invite us to come with you, Manny?" asked Bouqueet. "The house has many places to hide. Together, we have a better chance to find them."

"Well, we know where George will be—in the pantry," said Alvin.

"If we all go, Mom and Dad will know. I didn't want to worry them," said Manny, though his tone reflected that he knew no one would agree to stay behind. "If you insist on coming, follow me as quietly as you can."

As the air became heavier, the clouds, dark with rain, prematurely dimmed the day's light. Manny had timed it right. They'd have the cover of darkness for crossing the open field just before the rain came. "Follow me," he said.

The open field ahead looked barren and unprotecting. A breeze turned the scarecrow with the worried face toward him, and Manny thought it looked sympathetic. They arrived at the foot of the scarecrow just as the wind carried the first raindrops as tears to the scarecrow's face. It offered shelter. Manny led the way up among the straw under the shoulder pads of its jacket where it was warm and dry. The rain was sometimes hard, sometimes light, sometimes seeming to stop before picking up again. Its staccato brought sleep.

* * *

In Manny's dream, Zeus observed a family of hungry mice being turned away from a garden of delicious food by two scarecrows. The scarecrows were dancing and cackling, waving their arms, and behaving generally in such a frightening way that the mice, despite being near starvation, were afraid to enter the garden and eat the food that lay just a few feet away.

"Please," said the mother to the scarecrows, "we don't eat much. Look at my children; they're too weak and hungry to go on. Please, if you will just let us eat a little today, we promise never to come back. No, no, don't swing that broom at us, please."

Zeus landed between the mice and the scarecrows. "What is this nonsense?" he asked, addressing the scarecrows. "Your job is to protect the food from birds and rabbits, not mice. Mice hardly eat enough for the farmer to notice. The mice need food, and I will lead them to it, no matter how much motion you make. So, don't bother to wear yourselves out, dancing around on those poles. It's way too embarrassing for you to be trying to scare mice. Everyone in the neighborhood will be laughing at you."

"And just who are you, anyway?" asked one of the scarecrows. "I don't remember the farmer saying anything about taking orders from any mouse. My orders are to move around in every breeze. I make no distinction. The farmer didn't say to frighten some creatures and not others. I don't make judgments about who is allowed in, who needs food, who will eat more than whom. No sir, none of that. That's not my job."

"Yeah," said the other scarecrow, "that's right. Orders are orders, and our orders are for indiscriminate discrimination. We don't like nobody, especially nobody who don't look more or less like us, which is the best way to look, as far as I know. Our purpose here is to make sure that everybody knows they're not welcome, and that includes you mister busybody, whoever you are."

"Who I am is not important," responded Zeus. "The problem here is that you do not know who *you* are. You are scarecrows. You have a very limited assignment for which you are well suited. It would be best if you understood what that was and stuck with it. That is the way to feel good about yourselves. Understand what you are good at, and do it."

"But we *are* good at keeping animals and birds out of the garden!"

"Some of them, yes. But you are not here to protect the garden from mice. Is the fence mouse-proof? Of course not.

Nothing but embarrassment will come to you if you try to assume responsibility for keeping mice out of the garden. Failing at that will not go unnoticed by the rabbits and birds. As soon as they observe that you have attempted and failed to keep out the mice, your gig is up. Nobody will give you any respect. The rabbits will be dancing among the cabbages right under your noses, and the birds will be sitting on your heads and doing what everyone knows birds do when they sit on you. It will not be a pretty or pleasant-smelling sight.

"I am going to lead these mice right into the garden. They are going to eat as much as they want and leave when they are full. And if you want to preserve your jobs, you will adopt a supercilious air that announces to any rabbit or bird who might notice that you are above concern for what mice do in the garden, because their needs are so small as to not merit the exercise of your considerable and valued skills at deterrence. Is that clear?" said Zeus, grabbing one of the scarecrows by the shoulder and pulling out a huge fist-full of straw.

"Well, I, I, I guess, so. I mean we wouldn't want to waste our talents—especially on mice, being so little and insignificant as they are," said the first scarecrow.

"Yes, I think I agree—particularly on the importance and value of our skills. That's hard to argue with, when you put it that way, I guess," said the second scarecrow. "I think I'll just take a rest here. The wind seems to have died down anyway, and I'm ready for a nap." The scarecrow yawned loudly and folded into himself as the wind came to a complete halt.

12. Alvin's Practical Joke

Silence woke Manny. There was no sound of wind or rain. There was complete darkness. "Wake up," he said, nudging first Alvin and then Bouqueet and Shyleen.

The house was a barely visible black image on an only slightly less black canvas of lightless sky that made the house seem more distant than Manny knew it was. Their journey was quick: to the crack in the foundation, into the crawlspace, and up the drain-pipe to the kitchen sink cabinet where the garbage smelled bad, as usual, and the mouse trap offered a contrastingly delicious-smelling cheese.

"No," said Manny, as Alvin started toward the trap. "You can eat after we find George and Caressa. You and Bouqueet start in the kitchen. Shyleen and I will go to the living room."

In the living room, Manny noticed a movement under the couch. It was a mouse. Caressa? It's you isn't it? What happened to you?"

Caressa was holding one leg off the ground. She had three wounds that were scabbed over and two longer ones that had not completely healed. Her hair was messed up, and she looked thin.

"I was under the silk, but Flora found me. She played rough until a loud noise distracted her. She and everyone else left the bedroom. I hid in a shoe under the bed. When they came back, they seemed to have forgotten about me."

"I'll get you out of here. Is your leg broken?"

"I don't think so. I'm so glad you came, Manny."

"Follow me. Shyleen, tell Alvin and Bouqueet we found Caressa."

In the kitchen, they all hugged Caressa, gently, and said how glad they were to see her. Shyleen cried a little.

"What about George?" asked Manny, looking at Alvin and Bouqueet.

"He wasn't in the pantry," said Alvin.

"The other place to hide is under that thing over there that's making noise and vibrating. I was afraid to look under it," said Bouqueet.

"Keep looking. I'll help Caressa get out of here," said Manny.

Under the kitchen sink, Manny slid down the pipe and held on tight just below the floor, so that he could help support Caressa as she slid down using only her three good legs. "Wait here," he said, and went back up the pipe.

He could hear his siblings' voices coming from the living room.

"You're a genius, Alvin," said Shyleen.

"Old Farmer Frank will never notice, probably," laughed Alvin. "But just imagine him puffing on his pipe and raising an eyebrow of suspicion that there's something a tad different about the tobacco."

"I think you're wasting your time," said Bouqueet. "It can't be a joke, if the butt of the joke doesn't know it's happening. I mean, it's funny to us, because we know about it, but what if Farmer Frank doesn't notice? *You* think he'll recognize he's been played a terrible trick, but if he can't smell any difference, he'll just smoke his pipe like every other time. So it won't be funny."

"It doesn't matter if that's what happens," said Shyleen. "We won't be here anyway. It's funny enough just imagining it. I see him lighting his pipe and drawing in a long, slow lung full of smoke without a clue. In fact, it's funnier to imagine him just smoking the pipe as though nothing is different." Shyleen was laughing uncontrollably.

As Manny came into the room, he saw Alvin leap from the arm of the couch to a glass-topped table and onto a long, narrow silk Persian carpet hanging on the wall next to a bookcase. Climbing the carpet, Alvin was able to grab onto a piece of colorful braided material that hung from the top of the bookcase and climb to the fourth shelf where Farmer Frank kept his pipe and pipe tobacco.

"What are you doing up there? We don't have time to be joking around," said Manny, sensing that Alvin was courting disaster.

"Wait till I tell you the joke. You'll die laughing. I'm going to deposit some droppings in the tobacco. Old Farmer Frank inhaling the sweet smell of mouse turds. It's too much. Just imagine the change of expression crossing his face. Will he show confusion, anger, nothing?"

Manny knew it was pointless to argue. No one would leave until Alvin came down, mission accomplished.

The bowl of the pipe was hooked over the top of the tin of tobacco, and the stem hung down, resting on the shelf. Alvin climbed up the stem of the pipe and reached out to grab the rim of the tobacco tin. As he did, the bowl of the pipe moved and slipped from the edge of the tobacco tin. Alvin managed to hang onto the tin's top edge with his front legs, but the pipe fell, bounced once, and tumbled off the shelf.

Manny watched the pipe fall straight down and hit the dried flowers that leaned out of a glass vase on the third shelf. The vase tilted and turned sharply before slipping off the front edge of the shelf, spilling its contents, and falling straight down, down, down to the glass-topped table at the foot of the bookshelf. The noise was an explosion of sound. Manny leaped into the air. Glass flew everywhere.

"Who's there?" yelled Farmer Frank from the bedroom.

"Oh, my goodness gracious me," said Mrs. Frank pulling on the chord of the lamp. "It sounded like someone broke a window."

"Rusty!" yelled Farmer Frank. "Rusty! Come on boy!"

Manny heard Flora jump off the bed. He heard Rusty coming. He heard Farmer and Mrs. Frank coming. They all arrived essentially at the same moment. "It's those mice!" yelled Mrs. Frank, advancing with a broom in her hand.

Manny saw no escape. A cat, a dog, and two people were determined to prevent it—unless something completely unexpected took place. He dashed directly toward Mrs. Frank. "Run! Run as fast as you can," he yelled as he leaped onto the edge of Mrs. Frank's nightgown and scrambled toward her face.

It worked. Mrs. Frank fainted and crashed to the floor, dropping her broom directly on Flora, who howled, hissed, and turned in a circle trying to figure out what had happened. Farmer Frank fell to his knees to attend to Mrs. Frank, and Rusty started to lick her face.

Shyleen and Bouqueet ran for the protection of the kitchen cabinet with Manny one step behind and Flora in close pursuit. Reaching the center of the kitchen, Manny dodged sharply left to draw Flora his direction, and she lost just enough footing on the linoleum for Manny to put a couple of steps between them. That was all he needed. Shyleen and Bouqueet had reached the cabinet, and he dived under the refrigerator as Flora's paw knocked his tail aside. He was safe.

In the living room, Mrs. Frank sat up and pushed Rusty's face away. "Are you okay?" asked Farmer Frank.

"Yes, I'm fine, I think. I can't believe how brazen those mice are. Where did they go?"

"Flora chased them into the kitchen. Let's see if she caught one."

"From the looks of Flora, here," Mrs. Frank said, "the mice must be under the refrigerator."

"That's good," said Farmer Frank, "I'll just pull the refrigerator out from the wall. Flora may have a midnight snack, or I might just shoot a few of `em. I'm gettin' mighty tired of mice eating the cheese from the traps."

"Oh, don't be talking nonsense," said Mrs. Frank. "You'll not be doing any shooting in my house. Hand me that yardstick. I can knock the mice out from under there when you pull the refrigerator away from the wall."

13. George's Nest

Manny saw the refrigerator starting to move above him, opening up a space by the wall. He moved with the refrigerator, keeping in the middle and out of reach.

"Psst, up here," said a familiar voice.

Manny looked up, and there in the middle of the cooling coils of the refrigerator was a nest with a mouse looking down at him. It was George. The tip of his tail was missing. "George, what are you doing up there?"

"Just get up here. It's the best hiding place in the house. You're never more than a few steps from food! I love it here."

The nest was made of material, one piece of which hung down like a rope for climbing into the nest. Manny climbed up. Mrs. Frank was banging the yardstick around under the refrigerator, and Flora was trying to get her nose far enough under to see something. But she couldn't.

"Get ready with the broom," said Mrs. Frank. "Flora will get the first mouse, but she'll need help if there's more than one."

From George's nest among the refrigerator coils, Manny and George watched the action below them, watched the yardstick pass back and forth, and waited. "Why didn't you come home?" Manny asked George, at last.

"Well, Flora never left the kitchen that night, so I was stuck here all the next day, as well. The second night, I intended to go home. But I was starved, so I stayed to have some cheese and crackers, a little cereal, some rice, a bite of dried apricot, another of prune—they cause gas, but they're really sweet—a little pasta, some raw brown sugar. Delicious! And chocolate too! That's pretty much the story. Every day I think I'll go home, but the food's so easy here."

Manny noticed that George had put on weight. He had distinct jowls. His belly looked like it wouldn't be far off the ground when he walked. "Mom and Dad will really be glad to see you."

"I'm … I'm not going back to the woodpile—at least not to live. I'm going to live here in the house. I've asked Maggie to be my wife. So far, she's holding back. But I've built this nest in case she changes her mind. What do you think of my nest? I found this stretchy material that Mrs. Frank puts her legs in to keep warm. It may be the only mouse nest like it in the whole world."

"It's a great nest, George."

"I don't see why anyone would want to live in the fields when being a house mouse is so much easier."

Farmer Frank's voice interrupted. "Those mice have got to be under that refrigerator. I'll just tip it slightly, so Flora can get under there and grab 'em."

"Don't you dare!" shouted Mrs. Frank. "Let's go back to bed."

"I'm wide awake now. I'd be lying in bed thinking about those greedy little mice thinking they got away with eating me out of house and home. Flora doesn't need much space to get under there. I'm going outside to get a board."

"I am *not* going to stay here to watch this. Before you so much as tip that refrigerator even an inch, you take everything out of it, so nothing spills. I'm going to bed."

Manny considered their situation. Flora was still waiting for them, and Farmer Frank's voice had a determined tone. The escape route under the kitchen sink was close by. With even a small element of surprise, Manny thought he would make it. But George was carrying extra weight and had no noticeable leg muscles. "George, we need to get ready to run. Do you remember how to get out of the kitchen?"

"Of course, I'm the world's expert on this kitchen. We could swing by the pantry and grab some food on the way out."

"You do and you'll be swinging from the end of a cat claw. This is serious, George. Just fly straight for the cabinet with the pipe to freedom."

Even as he said it, Manny knew George would not be "flying" anywhere. Manny would have to distract Flora by running in the opposite direction and making a quick cut-back. He just needed enough separation to make it a short foot-race. For Flora, this wasn't a survival contest. That would be the difference.

Farmer Frank went outside but quickly returned. He kneeled down to look under the refrigerator. Manny could feel his body heat and smell his breath: traces of onion, potatoes, some kind of dead animal, and toothpaste. It smelled awful. A board came sliding under one side of the refrigerator, which started to lift off the ground, raising a clank and clatter from inside.

"Oh no!" said Farmer Frank in a suppressed tone. "I forgot to remove the bottles."

Farmer Frank removed the bottles and closed the refrigerator door. George and Manny saw the end of the board come sliding under the refrigerator beneath them and watched it raise the refrigerator off the ground on one side.

"Get 'em, Flora!" whispered Farmer Frank, lifting the refrigerator just a little higher. Flora stuck her head underneath with her nose pointed straight to where Manny and George were hiding in the pantyhose nest. Her paw raked the legging hanging down.

Manny and George waited as the nest rose up at an angle. Suddenly, the refrigerator lost its footing, slipped, and fell through the glass of the rear kitchen door. Shattering glass, splintering wood, and buckling metal broke the air as the refrigerator came to rest catawampus at a 45 degree angle with its upper third extended outside the door to the porch. From outside, Dal barked.

"Jump," yelled Manny. George headed straight toward the sink cabinet. Manny feigned a step toward the pantry, hoping to confuse Flora. It didn't work. Flora had George pinned to the linoleum before he had taken his third step and sank her teeth into his flesh from both sides.

Manny watched, stunned by the sound of teeth slicing flesh and crushing bones. He made a move toward them, but the low growl in Flora's throat held him in place. Flora clamped her jaw down even tighter. Manny was only inches from them. He watched George's eyes close and heard his lungs struggling to expand for air. He moved closer, daring Flora to drop George for a second prize. But his presence seemed only to make her more determined. She watched Manny, but kept her jaw locked on George.

Almost no time had elapsed since the crash of the refrigerator through the door, but Flora's jaw trapped the ticking seconds as tightly as it clamped down on George. Manny watched, unable to take a breath himself as he waited for George to breathe, waited for Flora to release George, waited for another chance to distract her from George. But George's eyes closed, his feet stopped kicking, and he did not inhale another whiff of air.

When Flora finally released her jaw, George's lungs seemed to fill, but no exhale followed. His legs twitched once and went still. Flora gave him a light flip with her paw, but George lay dead still. Manny hesitated, helpless, hopeless. Rusty stood wide-eyed and looked at Farmer Frank as though waiting for instructions or more entertainment. Farmer Frank stood with the board in his hands, staring at the catawampus refrigerator and no longer saying anything.

"What on earth is going on out there!" yelled Mrs. Frank, interrupting the now silent drama, the still-life painting of players on a stage, and releasing Manny to slip into the cabinet before Flora could react. He slid down the pipe to where Caressa was waiting.

"Manny, it's you!" Caressa whispered. "What was that noise up there? The whole house shook."

"I'll tell you later. Where are Bouqueet and Shyleen?"

"I told them to go on ahead, so they could get to the protection of the fence-line before daylight."

Manny thought of George lying without a breathing motion, without a sign of life. He decided not to tell Caressa about him just yet. "It will be light soon. Let's get some rest."

Caressa was soon asleep. Manny was tired, but not sleepy. He lay listening to the considerable noise above them where Farmer Frank righted the refrigerator and boarded up the smashed kitchen door.

Manny thought how his mother's face would light up when she saw Caressa. But, of course, he'd have to tell her what had happened to George. Would he have to tell her that George had decided to live in the house? No, he decided that could be his secret. He would tell her, instead, how George had escaped the first time by hiding under the refrigerator and how he had built a nest from an unusual piece of human clothing. That was clever, really. And he had made friends with the house mice and learned some useful skills from them. He would tell his parents the things that would make them proud of George.

They slept until early evening. The Franks were moving about in the kitchen. Rusty was wolfing down dried dog food and dropping bits and pieces on the floor. The refrigerator was running. Manny wondered if they'd removed George's nest. It seemed to take forever, but eventually, the lights went out.

"I'm going back to find George and Alvin," Manny said, keeping secret that finding George meant finding his body.

"Why don't we just wait here? If they're okay, they have to come out this way."

"I won't be gone long," Manny said and disappeared up the pipe.

14. Choices

Inside the kitchen sink cabinet, Manny saw a mouse's tail with its tip missing sticking out from behind the garbage pail. "Is that you, George?" he whispered, unbelieving.

There was no answer. The tail did not move. Behind the pail, George was lying with his feet straight in the air. He looked peaceful. Manny sat beside him, thinking. *Things didn't always work out to escape. He didn't always come up with something clever enough, something fast enough. Zeus had not fired a thunderbolt to save George.*

He rolled his brother onto his side, so he would not look quite so dead, or more comfortable, or something. On his side, George looked like he was just sleeping. Manny remembered that George had made fun of him for being small. He had hated that. But he loved finding George under the refrigerator.

Mice grow up fast. They were no longer children. They could accept each other as brothers, but also as different and special to each other for who they were. George's teasing did not seem important now. Looking at his brother, he decided that he would be more tolerant of the house mice. *Probably, it isn't wrong to live in a house. Maybe it isn't better to live in a field*, he thought. He felt tired. He felt like his father, worried, and grateful to have escaped one more time.

He squeezed out of the warped cabinet door. The kitchen was dark. No light was coming from any room. He was almost to the living room door when he heard a mouse coming. "Alvin, is that you?" he asked.

"No, it's me, Maggie. George, is that you?"

Oh no, thought Manny. *It's the mouse George was trying to convince to be his wife.* "Hello, Maggie, it's me, Manny, George's brother. I'm looking for our other brother, Alvin. George isn't here right now."

"Where did George go?"

"Did you hear the noise last night, the breaking glass and the crashing sound?"

"Yes, what was it?"

"Farmer Frank tipped the refrigerator to help the cat catch George and me in his nest under there. I guess you know about the nest."

"Yes, I've seen it, but I don't like it. The refrigerator is noisy. So you and George were under the refrigerator when Farmer Frank tipped it over?"

"Unfortunately, we were, and Flora was right on us. George never had a chance." Manny felt bad that he had just blurted it out. "Flora just bit hard and held on. She didn't try to play with him—nothing like that. She just kept her jaw clamped until every bit of life was gone. There was nothing I could do."

Manny paused and looked at the ground. Maggie was stunned. "I'm sorry," she said. "George just wanted to live in the house. Just wanted to be accepted. He was a good mouse. I..."

"I think having you as his friend made him happy. That was enough for him." Manny hugged Maggie and paused before continuing, "Do you know where Alvin is? I need him to help me take George's body out to the field."

Maggie felt doubly bad—bad that George had been caught by Flora and bad that she had not tried to change his mind about having a nest under the refrigerator. "Why do you want to take George's body out to the field?" she asked at last.

"It's a field mouse custom. We place the body in the open to be sure that it contributes to the life of another creature. Don't house mice do that?"

"No. When a mouse dies, we leave the body for Mrs. Frank to find. We want her to think Flora is responsible. You see, Flora is not really a particularly good mouser. We wouldn't want Mrs. Frank to think Flora wasn't doing her job and get more or different cats. Here's Alvin," she said, turning as Alvin came through the door.

"Manny? What are you doing here? Come back for some more food, did you? Well, I was heading for the pantry myself. Come join me. Isn't Maggie the cutest mouse? Just look at her hair. It's as silky smooth as you find. It's the butter, I think. Will you join us for a midnight snack?"

"I didn't come here to eat," said Manny. "I came to make sure you were all right. Caressa is waiting under the house. We need your help to get George's body out to the field."

"George's body? What happened to George?"

"I'll tell you the story later."

"I'll help too," said Maggie.

Manny led them to where George lay on his side just as he had left him. They eased him to the edge of the opening beside the pipe. Manny and Alvin held onto the pipe just below the floor while Maggie tipped George into the hole. His stomach barely fit through the opening, so that he slid slowly, giving Manny a chance to brace for the weight and for Alvin to grab a leg in time to keep the body from falling away from the pipe. Still, it was not a graceful descent. In the end, they lost control, and George fell the last foot to the ground.

Even Caressa helped a little as they dragged George well away from the house to the open field where his body was sure to be found on his first night—by an owl, a raccoon, a vulture.

Maggie was thinking about how she had not had the courage to tell George she was not going to marry him. There was no spark there. She was nice to him and had told him she admired the ingenuity of his nest. But she had not wanted to share his nest with him, and now she was glad she had not told him that. He died, thinking he had made the perfect nest for them. That was okay. It was a clever nest—just in the wrong place and for the wrong mate.

They stood holding hands beside the body. Manny was trying to remember what Moses had said about the meaning and purpose of life when Macon died. In the end, he said, "We commit our brother to the nurture of life. His death becomes life." Then he started the chant and the others joined in.

Spirit to body, body to spirit,
Life to death, death to life again.

Manny cut the chant short. "It's too dangerous for us to stay here. Maggie, I guess this is where we part. We'll be going to the woodpile."

"Not me," interrupted Alvin. "I'm hungry. I'm going back to the pantry."

"It'll be too late to get home safely if you go back to the pantry," said Manny.

"I don't intend to leave the house. I've decided to make it my home. Winnie, Maggie, and Mud will join me in quiet time for George right here in this house. His spirit is as much here as in the woodpile. Mother will understand. I'll come back to the woodpile to visit later. But not now. I want to wait and see the expression on Farmer Frank's face when he lights up his pipe. Give my love to Mom and Dad, and tell them I'm safe."

Manny gave Alvin a loving bump. "You be careful in that house, brother. The Frank's may not appreciate your humor."

Manny and Caressa started across the pasture toward the fence-line, the night wind startling their warm bodies and urging them to quicken their pace. Reaching the protection of the tall weeds, Manny looked back. Despite its imposing size against the sky, the house no longer looked threatening.

It was familiar now. The worried scarecrow with the furrowed brow, his suit filled out by the wind and the lines in his face softened by distance, also looked more friendly, as if he might say, "Come any time you want. We don't mean you no harm." The garden looked peaceful, inviting. And, although he could not see her face, he knew the scarecrow at the far end was smiling.

Manny watched Caressa run—hobble—past him. "There's no hurry now. We have good cover the rest of the way. Let's take a rest," he said.

Manny was mentally tired. He thought about George's nest and his intent to get married. Manny didn't feel ready for that yet. The more he learned, the more questions he seemed to have.

The sky was dark. No stars. No moon. The air was humid, heavy. Manny listened to the wind rustle through the heavy grass. "We should go. It smells like rain."

"I'm ready," said Caressa, but she moved awkwardly, touching her swollen leg down only lightly. "Do you know where we are?"

"It's not much farther. We're almost to the pear tree. We can rest again there."

A bramble of flowering raspberry vines at the foot of the pear tree was thick and a safe place to rest. Manny looked at his sister. She was tired, but there was something more. "What's the matter?"

"Oh, it's nothing. I was just feeling sad about the silk. I wanted to be the only one to have a nest lined with silk. I know it's selfish and vain, but I can't help it. I want it. Do you think it would be crazy for me to go back and try again? After my leg is healed, I mean."

"I'm not the right one to ask. I don't have any fire in me to possess silk. You know the dangers of going into the house, as well as I do."

Caressa thought about the silk. It was true. Manny didn't understand. *Maybe I could explain it to Mother,* she thought. *She'd understand. I got my love of cloth from the wool nest she raised us in. She wanted to have a wool nest. I want a silk one. Mother will love silk.*

They moved slowly along the fence to the woodpile, resting regularly, and finally crawled into the opening made by the warped boards. They dropped through the knothole, followed the hallway of the hollow tree-trunk, and proceeded on down through the paths in the rotted wood to their family's wool-lined nest. They snuggled in among their sleeping family.

* * *

In Manny's dream, Zeus was having a busy night, exacerbated by the antics of Mud, also known as Triple M and as Marvelous Maxwell Mouse. There were many mice to look after, and Zeus resented that Mud was requiring so much attention.

On this night, Mud was intent on provoking a fight between Flora and Rusty. He ran directly between them while they were eating. Flora's nerves were always taut when her bowl was put out at the same time as Rusty's. She felt it insulting to have to eat in the vicinity of that slobbering animal. So, on the sight of the mouse, Flora pretended to make a swipe at it while, in reality, aiming her claw directly at, and landing in, the nose of Rusty.

Shocked, the poor dog knocked over the water dish. For Flora, this was the last straw. In fact, she had recently been reduced to drinking out of the toilet bowl, because the Franks were putting out only one water dish. There was no way Flora was going to share a water dish with Rusty. With the water now running under her dainty paws, Flora, furious, clawed Rusty again. Seeing his success, Mud stopped to laugh, instead of making a hasty retreat, and found himself trapped in the corner, facing an angry cat, a dog with hurt feelings, a woman with a broom, and a man with a shotgun. There was no escape.

Zeus was forced to intercede, landing just in time to shield Mud and—to their total amazement—address the standing army of Flora, Rusty, Farmer Frank, and Mrs. Frank.

"If you please," Zeus said. "Although I fully agree that a solid dose of punishment is in order, you seem to have the lethal kind in mind, which is against my principles in all cases, and in this case, in particular, since I hope we can all agree that the offense is more petty than felonious."

Rusty, Flora, Farmer Frank, and Mrs. Frank were too shocked to respond, facing, as they were, this small, though powerfully built mouse with a jagged white mark that looked like lightning on his chest and bearing a rod that he brandished in a way that suggested authority and power. But at length, Flora blurted out, "Well, it's easy enough

for you, whoever you are, to call it petty, but there is such
a thing as dignity, a condition we cats were put on earth
to guard. Goodness knows there'd be none at all on the
planet if its defense were left to the dogs. I don't know what
the punishment for causing indignity is where you come
from, but, personally, I'm not convinced that it should not
be lethal."

"I could just slobber all over him, maybe," said Rusty.
"Would that be an acceptable punishment?"

"That might be worse than a slow death," muttered
Flora.

"How about if I attach him to the clothesline by his tail
and leave him to contemplate how long he'll last before an
owl or a hawk spies him?" asked Mrs. Frank. "He might just
die from the thought of it. That seems appropriate after all
the times he's tried to scare me to death."

Zeus could see that reason was not going to prevail.
He considered what punishment might suit the offense—
something involving Mud's humiliation in front of the mice
who would take shelter in the house in winter, for example.
But would this assembly of executioners recognize mouse
humiliation? It was a terrible dilemma, and Zeus could feel
a headache coming on.

* * *

Manny awoke. Only his mother and Caressa were still in the
nest. His mother was cleaning Caressa's hair. "You slept a
long time," she said.

"We've been talking about George and Alvin," said Caressa.

"Caressa told you what happened to George?" asked Manny.

"Yes."

Manny saw that his mother had been crying, that she looked sad, maybe older. He did not know what to say. What could he say that would make a difference?

"It's hard to let children find their own way," his mother said after awhile.

"Maybe Alvin will get married and bring his children to see us. I'll show them all the good things to eat out here in the fields," she added with forced cheerfulness.

"Alvin will be all right, mother," said Manny. "He's funny. Everybody likes him, and the house is really not very dangerous. The cat and the dogs are well fed. Farmer and Mrs. Frank seem to be deliberately feeding the mice."

"You must be hungry, Manny. Why don't you go out and find something to eat? Tonight, we'll have special time together in memory of George."

* * *

That night, the family remembered George. "It's not fair. George didn't really have a chance," said Bouqueet.

"Yeah," chipped in Shyleen, "why do cats get nine lives? Cats don't seem to face anything more dangerous than heartburn from being fed too much. Mice are the ones who need nine lives. Even two would have been enough for George."

"Cats don't really have nine lives," said Martha, their mother. "They have one life like every other creature. In the wild, they probably experience many close calls, just as we do. I didn't want George to live in the house, but he lived where he wanted to. That was a good thing."

Manny described how clever George's nest was. "The material was really soft but strong. You might have been jealous, Caressa."

They talked about George's favorite foods, like chocolate, until everyone began to drift off, except Martha and Manny. Martha lay hugging George's spirit and humming the lullaby that George thought he was too old for.

Manny lay troubled, but by what, he couldn't say. He felt the need for something to change in his life without knowing what it was he wanted. He felt the answer was inside him, waiting to be freed, waiting for action or reaction, waiting for a thought unknown to him, waiting to be revealed to him.

But the answer remained hidden. He was a sailboat calm in the water before the storm. He could smell the storm forming, but there was, as yet, no wind for the sail. For now, he was incapable of anything, except the excitement and dread of anticipation.

15. Alvin and Maggie Pay a Visit

Manny, Caressa, Shyleen, and Bouqueet were on Manny's porch in the early evening as cold became the absence of heat and sent them in search of the warmth of the family's wool nest.

"Guess who's come for a visit," said Martha as they entered. "Alvin and Maggie are here."

Manny ran over and gave Alvin a hard body bump. "You look great. Life must be treating you well at Farmer Frank's."

"You mean his stomach looks full, right?" said Maggie, laughing. "It's okay. He's very comfortable to rest my head on. And now that he knows there's always more food than he needs, he's getting more choosey—although, as we know, chocolate still buckles his knees."

"Look at Manny's leg muscles, Alvin," said Caressa.

"He's bigger than I am," said Shyleen. "In fact, I think he's as tall and long as you, Alvin. He's just not as round."

"Well, I guess we're all growing up," said Alvin, trying to sound indifferent to the subject of whether his brother had really caught up to him.

"Alvin," said Maggie, as if to help him out. "Tell everyone what happened when Farmer Frank lit his pipe."

"I forgot all about that," said Caressa. "Did you see him light his pipe?"

"Oh yeah," said Alvin, moving his ears up and down. "The first thing I smelled was him stuffing the tobacco into the pipe. Rusty was curled up at his feet, looking like he was down for the night. Anyway, Farmer Frank settled into his chair, pulled out the lighter, and fired it up. I'm hiding there about to bust a gut, waiting for the look of contentment on his face to change."

"I was watching too," interrupted Maggie. "I was sure that as soon as he smelled something wrong in the tobacco, he'd come looking for us."

"Well, anyway," said Alvin, "humans don't seem to smell things the way we do. I don't know why I thought he'd notice. The smoke rolled out of his mouth and nose— even his ears, it seemed like. And he just looked like he was enjoying the most fragrant pipe-full of tobacco he'd ever had. Who knows? Maybe to a human, mouse droppings in the tobacco give it just the spicing the stuff needs."

"Goodness knows," added Maggie, "it smells foul enough *without* mouse droppings in it."

"So nothing happened?" asked Bouqueet.

"No, no, something happened all right. I was just getting to that," continued Alvin. "Farmer Frank was puffing away as if the tobacco was particularly good when old Rusty raised his head and started to sniff the air like something wasn't quite right. He sniffed and sniffed. He raised himself up with his nose pointing toward the smoke, looking agitated and even barked—not loud, but quiet like he was onto something."

"Farmer Frank must have thought Rusty heard something outside," interrupted Maggie, "because he got up out of his chair, went outside, and took Rusty with him. So, it sort of turned out to be a joke on Rusty, instead of on Farmer Frank."

"I thought it was pretty funny," said Alvin, "even if it didn't happen like it was supposed to. You had to be there though."

"It is a little funny, I guess," said their mother. "I just hope you'll be careful with your pranks. Lots of creatures would be looking to get even with a mouse who's played a trick on them."

"Maggie," said Bouqueet, to change the subject, "did you finish your nest? You were making it with the stuffing from the living room chair, right?"

"Yes," interrupted Alvin, "it's the most comfortable nest in the whole house; it's completely safe; and it's heated, too."

"Where is it?" asked Shyleen.

"It's on top of the heating duct under the kitchen. I helped her build it."

"When the heat comes on," interjected Maggie, "the duct keeps us warm now, it'll be cool under there in the summer, and it's a safe place too."

"And the best part," said Alvin, excitedly, "is that we're close to the pantry. Location, location, location," he said with extra emphasis, as though he'd coined the phrase. "Can't beat it."

"So, if you two built a nest together, you must be married?" interrupted Martha with a questioning tone and a surprised look.

"Yes, that's what we came to tell you, actually," said Maggie in a matter-of-fact and proud tone.

"Married?" shouted Shyleen, Caressa, and Bouqueet at the same time.

"How could you do that without us?" asked Bouqueet

"Wow, that's great, Alvin," said Manny, giving him such a hard body bump it knocked him onto his side.

Alvin recovered and was set to reciprocate when Maggie stepped between them. "In the house, mice get married by building a nest together. Isn't that how you get married in the field?"

"Of course not," said Bouqueet. "To get married, you have to have a celebration. Everybody comes. You have a feast and a ceremony. You can't just build a nest and be married."

"Well, never mind about what we do," said Martha, their mother. "In the house, they do things different. Different isn't wrong. It's just different. And Maggie and Alvin are a wonderful couple. And they are here. So, we get to do things the field mouse way. Girls, spread the news and start gathering food. We'll have a proper feast here in the hollow tree-trunk."

And they did. Everyone brought something. The children played hide and seek. The adults ate too much and told stories that stretched the truth. A few mice made comments about Maggie being a house mouse and about Alvin taking up the easy life next to the pantry.

"It's all right, of course," said Moses, "to go into the house in the middle of the winter when it can be hard to keep warm and find enough food out here. It's a survival thing. But once the snow is gone, it's not natural."

"Especially, to live there permanently," chipped in a neighbor. "Who wants to live next to a cat and a dog? I don't care how much food there is or how easy it is to find. You wouldn't find me living in a house."

"It's just not what we're used to," said Martha. "Just because the house seems strange to us, doesn't mean it's not a good place to live. Anyway, Maggie seems like a wonderful mouse. She's teaching Alvin about nutrition. I think they'll bring me very healthy grand children. Who could find fault with that?"

"Martha's right," said Louise. "My brother married a house mouse, and they are very happy. They have lots of children, too."

No one was convinced, of course, but no one wanted to spoil the evening either. So the conversation turned to children, the weather, and the locations of fruit, nuts, grain, and herbs until everyone had eaten more than enough, everyone had toasted the bride and groom, and everyone drifted off to their nests.

16. The Hawk

It was late afternoon when Manny slipped out of the nest and onto his porch. He needed time alone to think. Something was changing inside him. He felt the urge for adventure, for danger. He wanted to enter the garden at the feet of the scarecrow with the smile and eat a carrot right under Dal's nose. Or a piece of cheese right under Rusty's and Flora's noses.

The sun had settled behind the hills, leaving colors and shadows that sharpened otherwise unnoticed details—a beautiful evening for running. Manny ran south of the woodpile, past the wild turkey nest and the leaning fence post, past the tall oaks from where the eyes of the raccoons sometimes watched, and down toward a small pond at the lower end of the pasture. Eight deer and a flock of wild turkeys were grazing next to the pond as Manny lay watching from the weeds.

The turkeys were the first to startle, quickly running and flying in anxious retreat. In the direction from which they had spooked, Manny saw a bobcat coming toward the pond.

It had a sleek gray coat and sharp pointed ears. Its face was flat and its yellow/green eyes scanned hungrily in every direction. Manny ducked deeper into the cover of the weeds away from the pond. A bobcat would not play with you until you died. It would eat you in a single chomp.

The bobcat turned to pursue the turkeys, and Manny headed in the opposite direction. He was so intent on his position relative to the bobcat that he forgot to check the sky before entering an open area. It was too late.

The shadow of a large bird's wing flashed across him, and he dived back into the weeds, remembering how Rachel had saved him from the owl the night they'd gone to Farmer Frank's garden. Only there was no protection here, no friend, no hole, no log, nowhere but the weeds and grass, which were no match for the hawk that had spotted him. The almost silent swoosh of the hawk's wings was a sound composed without a note of hope. The hawk's talons grabbed him and lifted him straight into the air.

In that instant, Manny was too terrified to think of his parents, of his siblings, of Rachel, or even of death. Fear enveloped him—mind and body—as he waited for the pain with his eyes tightly closed. But the talons were wrapped around his body so that he felt only a little squished, not hurt, and he soon opened his eyes, watching the land fall away as the hawk flew higher and higher.

Looking down, he could see the mulberry, cherry, persimmon, dogwood, pear, and sassafras trees, the tall oaks, the small pond, and the woodpile. He could see Farmer Frank's house, the barn, and the smiling and care-burdened scarecrows. He could see Dal's house and the garden with its carrots and lettuce. Rusty and Dal were specks sitting on the porch. From up in the sky, the garden looked small— not at all as it had seemed the night he and Rachel had first gone there.

Manny was no longer afraid, though he knew he should be. Flying above the familiar landscape was like being Zeus, a creature of magic powers, surveying the world, poised to protect the life of every mouse.

The hawk squeezed him a little tighter, as if to remind him that he was not Zeus and that fantasy would not help him now. *What chance did he have to save himself? The hawk had not stopped to eat him. Did she intend to feed him to her babies?* he wondered, imagining blind hawk babies squawking with their mouths open, waiting for him as stomach-filler, a fearful image.

The hawk would drop him from close range. If he pumped his legs and twirled his tail, maybe he could affect where he fell. If the chicks were still young and blind, maybe he could escape before their mother could react. It wasn't much of a plan, but it was all he could think of.

As the hawk carried him higher and higher, Manny concentrated on the landmarks below. He watched as they passed across the southern part of the cornfield that was familiar to him. They passed over a hay field, a pasture with a lake, a grove of trees, and a large creek with a strong current, stirring the water white where there were rocks. Many trees, including several large sycamores, grew along the edge of the creek. The creek would be between him and home. He could not swim.

The hawk approached a tall tulip poplar tree that rose high in the air above the other trees at the base of the Blue Ridge foothills. Manny could see her nest, and the hawk rose gracefully above where it rested in the tree's uppermost branches.

The nest below him was a miniature world of horrors where five vulturous carnivores screamed for his body in a nest reeking of foul breath, of bird poop, of feathers, of blood, and of death. The stench was nauseating and he held his breath.

Manny tensed his muscles, bracing for the coming assault. He took a deep breath and another and another, preparing for the split second when he would be released from the hawk's grasp and dropped to the deadly mouth of a baby hawk.

The babies were screeching at a high, ear-piercing pitch. Manny blocked out the noise. One more deep breath. And it happened. The talons released him so close and low that the heat of the intended baby's breath rose up to meet him as the mouth opened.

Manny kicked as hard as he could. His powerful legs and tail kicked and jerked and gave him just enough movement to avoid a direct landing in the intended baby bird's beak. He kicked the side of the beak and jumped clear as it snapped shut. He fell into the nest among the blind birds and thrust his legs with such force that he was half-way up the side of the nest before the babies could react and only one beak got a nip at his tail before he leaped to the edge of the nest and down around under it to one of the branches on which the nest rested.

The mother hawk, expecting her babies to be squabbling over the mouse instead of shrieking to be fed, looked confused when there was no relief from her babies' pleading until she saw Manny's tail disappear over the edge of the nest. She lifted her powerful wings and hovered in the air away from the nest, seeking a line of sight, a flight-path to the escaping dinner for her chicks. But Manny climbed between two of the branches supporting the nest and wiggled in tightly among the twigs of the nest so that the hawk could not get at him or even see him.

The hawk came back around, scanning the nest and looked down on the ground. Maybe the mouse had fallen? She swooped down and glided around the area near the tree again and again. No movement. No sign of a mouse. She swooped back up and sat on one of the branches holding her nest. The babies pleaded. "Food, food, food, we're hungry." She rose up off the branch and resumed the hunt. There were many more mice in the fields.

From where he stayed hidden, the intensified screeching of the babies soon let Manny know that the mother hawk was returning. Each wanted to be the mouth to receive the gift. And one was. Manny heard one of the screeching babies silenced and felt sick. A mouse had been delivered.

But at least it was not him. He had a chance to escape this den of death. He just had to be patient. He tried to distract himself with thoughts of being Zeus, wielding lighting and thunder, but he couldn't. For one thing, he was not feeling particularly invincible, hiding inside the nest of the hawk, and for another, he couldn't block out the sounds above him—the mother hawk returning with clockwork regularity, announcing her arrival, and briefly silencing one baby's scream on each visit.

Burrowed deep among the nest's twigs and feathers, Manny initially failed to notice the slow advance of night. What he sensed first was the air growing heavy, cooling fast, and smelling of distant rain. Manny wanted to leap from the nest, watch the thunderheads roll in, and anticipate the first splashes washing his face and coat. Rain was always a blessing. It bore life, and tonight Manny would use it to save his.

The black thunderclouds extinguished the last of day's light, lit the nest with lightning, and rocked it with thunder. Zeus was his fantasy, but real lightning and thunder would save him. Manny could feel it. He could hear the rain advancing—a hard rain with large drops. He could hear the puddles sprouting.

The baby hawks' screeching, interrupted by each bolt of lighting and thud of thunder, reached a peak once more. The mother returned, silenced one baby, and then all of them. She settled into the nest, pulling the babies in under her large wings, just as the large tulip poplar leaves bent from the weight of the drops they'd blocked and released the water onto the nest. The hawk's heavy feathers shed the water easily and her body kept the babies warm.

With the nest gone quiet and the rain overpowering some of the smell, Manny could think. The night's dark had joined the black of the thunderheads to snuff out every trace of light. On the next flash of light, he shifted position and moved to the outermost twigs under the nest as the thunder rolled in behind. He sat with his nose looking out and waited for the next lightning strike. When it came, it was so close Manny could smell the fire. The thunder that boiled up from within the heart of the great tree shook every branch with fear.

It was just what Manny needed. He made his way from the forked, small branches that held the nest to the larger branch, the next larger, and the next. When the lightning lit again, it seemed as though every hawk within a hundred miles could see him—one small mouse gripping the bark of a branch rising from the trunk of this giant tulip poplar.

Manny dared not look up or down. He kept his eyes focused on the heavy bark, advancing down to the next branch and the next, without looking at the sky's flashing fire or reacting to the echoes of the sound waves that followed. He ran with the bark, following the rain's rivulets cascading within the crevices of the bark, following it down, down, down the massive tree-trunk to the safety of the earth.

He was half-way down the last twenty feet of trunk when the lightning fired again in one last attempt to expose his presence to every creature of ill intent that surely lay in wait for this innocent, escaping his sentence of death. Manny stopped for a quick look, and though he saw no immediate danger, the blackness of this unknown place was terrifying for what it surely failed to reveal. These Blue Ridge foothills harbored no friends of mice.

Manny dropped to the ground with the strike of thunder. He was exhausted and needed a place to hide. He started down the fence-line, looking for something that offered protection and a camouflaging smell. The bolts of lightning were welcome lanterns, though they were distant now and followed by more muted tympani, a vibration he could feel as much as hear. The rain had lost its storm and was settling into an all-nighter's comforting sound of droplets finding roots, grateful plants drinking, and color rising in the stems of every growing thing.

Manny followed the fence for a long time before he found a particularly dense growth of multiflora rosebushes and honeysuckle climbing a mulberry tree along the fence. He squeezed in and scanned the interior. It was better than he'd hoped. It was virtually impenetrable to any animal larger than a mouse. Best of all, a short, rotted section of a large tree branch lay inside. Manny dug a small nest in the end of the rotted branch and settled in to sleep, protected from the rain.

When he awoke, it was late afternoon the next day. The rain had stopped, and he was starved. He looked back in the direction of the poplar tree. It was not as far away as he had hoped. He scanned the sky and saw the hawk circling. If he was to get back to the woodpile, he would need to move mostly at night and play a successful game of run and hide when he moved by day. Run when the hawk was in its nest; hide when she was cruising for food. To the east, he could see the tall sycamore trees along the creek that lay between him and home.

As darkness approached, the air still smelled of the previous night's rain, though the cool of night was fast sucking its humidity. Manny loved running under those conditions. By dawn, he had almost reached the sycamores. He took cover and considered how to cross the creek that blocked his road home.

17. The Beavers

Whack! Whack! Whack! The noise rang out across the water, and an animal rushed through the grass and weeds in his direction. The whacking noise came from the water in front of him. The animal came from behind him. But the two seemed coordinated somehow. The animal was a beaver, headed straight for the water with no interest in him. Manny could see two beavers already in the water. The one that had passed by him was running south along the creek and yet another appeared from the trees and joined her. They slipped into the water and joined the two already there. They swam downstream and disappeared under the surface.

Manny knew beavers built dams. If they had one nearby, maybe he could use it to cross the creek and find his way to the woodpile. He ran downstream toward where the beavers had disappeared, keeping inside the weed-covered area off from the banks of the creek until he reached where the water slowed, no longer rushing and bubbling around the rocks, no longer bearing twigs hurriedly along its waves. Instead, it gathered itself and placed its twigs and leaves gently into the expanding pool behind the dam.

Manny waited. As soon as the hawk turned toward its nest, Manny ran for the dam. He was midway across when he saw that the dam did not reach the other side of the creek. Worse yet, Dal was on the other side drinking water and looking all too ready to chase whatever moved. There wasn't time to get back to the weeds before the hawk would return. The only escape was among the mud, branches, and twigs that made up the dam. He dug, squeezed, scratched and burrowed deeper and deeper inside the dam. He squeezed and wiggled and scratched, inching deeper and deeper until he fell in a heap from the ceiling of the beavers' living room and passed out. The beavers were quite surprised.

"What was that?" said Beatrice, looking up from her whittling.

"Well, I'll be," said Bernard, her husband. "It's a mouse."

"What's a mouse doing here?" asked Diana, their daughter.

"How did it get in here, anyway," asked their son, Daniel.

"He just fell out of the ceiling," said Beatrice. "Must've dug in from the top of the dam."

"Is he dead?" asked Diana.

"Seems to be breathing," said Bernard. "His chest is heaving, and I can see his heart pounding." Bernard was not happy. It's hard to say you've built an impregnable home, if a mouse gets into it.

"He could be carrying a strange disease," said Daniel.

"Don't be ridiculous," said Beatrice. "He's just an ordinary mouse. I wonder what was out there that scared him so badly?"

"Maybe he saw the Dalmatian. That's why I signaled for us to come home," said Bernard.

"Oh, Dad," said Daniel. "You made us come in just because of that dumb dog? If he's smart, he won't even think about chasing a beaver."

"There's no honor lost in waiting for the dog to leave. If you want to go out, stay in the water. Dogs are terrible swimmers. He'll tire quickly and go back to land. Speaking of being tired, I think this is the perfect time for a nap."

"Let's go, Diana. Maybe we can lure the dog into the water," said Daniel.

"Be careful!" yelled Beatrice as they turned to leave. Beatrice looked at Manny, who was breathing less heavily now, and marveled at this little creature with the muscular legs. *How did it make its way in the world?*

Beatrice worried about her children, but they had formidable natural gifts with which to protect themselves: powerful claws, teeth, and jaws. Even their tails could be weapons. And, of course, they were smart, endowed with engineering skills that set them apart from other animals. But this mouse looked completely defenseless.

Manny slept the rest of that day and all night. His body had catching up to do. Toward the next morning, he began to reach the state of dream sleep.

* * *

In Manny's dream, Zeus had not had a moment's rest for several days and nights. The number of mouse-eaters was multiplying. Everywhere Zeus looked, listened, or smelled, the information was not good. He flicked his magic rod just in time to protect a family of mice from being trampled by a bull, pawing aggressively for seemingly no reason next to a haystack where the mice had their nest.

"If you please, Mr. Bull," Zeus said as he zapped the startled animal with a bolt of electricity that sent its hair into a frizz, "why don't you look what you're doing? What's with this aggressive pawing? Did it ever occur to you that some creature on this earth other than you might need a bit of space? Now back off here and go fill one of your four stomachs with grass before I turn your horns into lightning rods and fry the space between them that you presume to be filled with brains."

Trying to see if his brains and horns were still in place, the bull rolled his eyes up toward the top of his head so far that only the whites were left showing. With his eyes rolled up and his hair frizzed out, he looked like a cartoon caricature.

"Well, I'm awfully sorry, Mr. Mouse, Sir," he said, looking remorseful and uncomfortable. "You see, I don't really do that aggressive pawing thing for the purpose of depriving anyone else of space. It's just something my mother taught me. You see, bulls are born with this anger that needs getting out every once in awhile, and Mother taught me and my brothers pawing as an alternative to our attempts to break each others' heads open. It seemed to work. I mean we butted heads a lot anyway, but at least sometimes we pawed the ground instead, so we managed to grow up somehow. My poor mother was only trying to lessen violence.

"I don't see how you get off—if you don't mind my saying so—criticizing my dear mother's approach to raising her children. I mean you seem to have this thing backward. I'm out here trying to avoid hurting someone—just like my mother told me—and you're accusing me—falsely I believe—of trying to deny living space to other creatures. I dare say it is not very nice to threaten to fry someone's brains with lightning either. And I believe any properly reared animal would also refrain from snide remarks regarding the presence of brains between others' horns. I can tell you that my brothers and I knocked brains regularly, so I know they're in there."

What have I done to deserve to be harangued by a bull who thinks himself a practitioner of non-violence and wants to lecture me on child-rearing, thought Zeus. "Never mind," he said. "I didn't mean that pawing the earth was completely bad. It's just that right there where you were about to do your pawing happens to be the nest of a family of ten mice. You would have smashed them. That's why I stopped you. And

I'm sorry about threatening to fry your brains. It's been a long day. If you'll excuse me, I need to be moving on."

Zeus made a move, hoping to leave before the bull could pontificate further, but another sizeable animal appeared to block his way.

* * *

Manny awoke to find Beatrice hovering over him. "It's okay," said Beatrice. "I won't hurt you. I'm a beaver. We don't eat mice. How do you feel?"

"I, I'm fine, I think. Where am I, and what did you say you were?"

"I'm a beaver, and you're in our home. This is my husband, Bernard. Our children, Diana and Daniel, are out swimming."

"Yes, now I remember. You must be the beavers who built the dam over the creek I was trying to cross."

"Did you say what your name was?"

"Manny. My name is Manny. I'm trying to get back to my family in the woodpile. I don't know exactly where it is, but I know the direction I need to go."

"You did some powerful digging to get down through the top of our dam," said Bernard. "No one is supposed to be able to enter our home except by diving under the water and coming through the chute. We beavers are excellent engineers, you know," Bernard added as though this assertion of competence would override the fact that a mouse had breached his dam.

"Yes, I know," said Manny. "My father told me about how you build dams."

"You must tell us about yourself," Bernard said to change the subject.

Manny told them about being caught by the hawk and how he'd escaped and about running and hiding. He explained how he'd used the creek and the sycamore trees as markers to guide him toward home. "I know the woodpile is toward where the sun rises, and it's a long ways away. But I'm faster than most mice, and I can run a long time at top speed. Do you run, much, Mr. Beaver?"

"Bernard, just call me Bernard. No, I don't run unless I think it's a good idea to get back to the water in a hurry. And I never go too far from the water. I like to know I can get back inside this impregnable fortress I built whenever..." Bernard paused and raised his eyes to the ceiling, looking annoyed and embarrassed.

"Do you know Farmer Frank and where his house is?"

"No, can't say that I do. Why do you want to know?"

"If I could find Farmer Frank's house, I'd know how to find the woodpile and my family's nest. There was a dog out along the bank of the creek when I arrived; did you see it?"

"Yes, of course. Why do you ask?"

"I know that dog. If he wandered here, it means I'm close enough that a dog who is not hunting for food ends up here just following his nose from one scent to another. But to get home, I need to get to the other side of the creek. So, I'll need to climb back up to the top of the dam."

"I'm afraid that's impossible. I built this dam. I know you got in, but that was down. Gravity is a powerful ally. Scratching your way upward would be a whole different story. Anyway, even if you got out of here—which you wouldn't, of course, because of how well I built this place— you'd just be on top of the dam, not on the other side of the creek."

"What do you mean?"

"The dam isn't above water the whole way. The other end of the dam is below the water level to let the water pass over the top. That keeps the level of our pond constant, so our home here doesn't get flooded and the water pressure doesn't build up and wash our dam away. Swimming is the only way to the other bank of the creek, and it's the only way out of our home. You don't swim, do you?" he asked, in a tone that was definitely smug.

"Now Bernard," interrupted Beatrice. "Look at Manny's legs. He obviously has a powerful kick. I'm sure he can swim through a stronger current than this creek."

"No," said Manny. "I can't swim at all. My legs are made for running." Manny felt as trapped as when he was caught in the hawk's talons, riding above the world, more confined than in the cabinet under Mrs. Frank's kitchen sink, more lacking a route for escape than when he was hiding in the hawk's nest. Nothing came to him. Swimming was not something his parents had mentioned as a survival skill, not something his father and Moses had talked about.

It was Beatrice who came up with the plan. "I know," she said. "Manny doesn't need to swim. He just needs to ride on your back while you swim to the other side of the creek."

"But wouldn't I drown? How will I breathe under water?"

"You won't," said Beatrice. "You can just hold your breath. That's what we do. We can hold our breath a long time. From running, your lungs must be strong too. It will be scary, since you've never done it before, but you can keep your eyes closed."

"I don't know," said Bernard. "What if the current pulls him off my back?"

"Just look at the strength in his legs and toes—a grip of steel, I'd say."

All Manny knew was that he wanted to get out of there. He was rested and eager to get on his way. "How long would I have to hold my breath?"

"Excellent question," said Beatrice. "Let's practice. When I say 'go,' you start holding your breath, and Bernard will imagine swimming out of here and yell 'stop' when he thinks enough time has passed. Go!"

"Stop," yelled Bernard in what seemed to Manny almost no time at all.

"That was easy. I could have held my breath much longer. I'm ready."

"Okay," said Beatrice. "Bernard, after you've dropped Manny at the other side of the creek, you could walk with him to the tree-line where he'll be shielded from the view of the hawk. It's not far and it's in the direction Manny is headed."

"Thank you very much. I don't know what to say. Thank you."

"We're just glad we're able to help."

"Absolutely," said Bernard, feeling a little heroic. "Hop aboard."

Manny ran up Bernard's broad tail and onto his back. He wrapped each of his toes firmly around clumps of the hair down at the roots. He felt nothing could dislodge him. "I'm ready," he said, and Beatrice waved good-by.

Manny took a deep breath and held it just as the water moved across his body. He tried to make himself open his eyes, but he couldn't until he felt them break the surface. For a moment, he forgot to breathe. Floating in the pond on Bernard's back was a trip so magical he had not even imagined it for Zeus. He had his own ship, gliding, parting the waters, waving the water, moving without effort.

There was nothing in this scene that Manny had not seen before. The line where water met land was populated with vines, weeds, and trees. The sky carried light clouds that did not shade the bright sun and held a few birds slowed in flight across its screen. But it was a sailor's vision—objects and landscape seen as they appear from the deck of a slow ship in a calm estuary—familiar but newly observed.

Of course, he'd watched birds and wished he could fly, so that even though he knew it was not something he could do, it was easy to imagine, to fantasize doing it. But to swim? It had not even been a thought, a wish; yet, now, it seemed possible.

"Stick close beside me and the hawk won't see you," said Bernard, interrupting Manny's thought. "I don't see her at this moment, but she's bound to be hunting."

They were an odd-looking pair: Bernard, walking with a deliberately slow gait, dragging his broad tail along the ground, and Manny, running full out to keep himself centered against Bernard's side until they were well in among the trees.

"Thank you," said Manny. "I can't thank you enough."

"Nothing, really. Best of luck to you."

Manny ran, freed from hiding and bound only by the limits of legs and lungs, the legs and lungs of an exceptional mouse, running for his life, for his home, for the fate knotted inside him, driving him to run.

18. Old Friend, New Friend

Manny did not stop to rest until evening light extended the shadows of the branches long to the east and the smell of chestnuts told him dinner was nearby. He was so tired he did not notice the other strong smell, bear poop, until he was almost on top of it. A mother bear and her cub had been there earlier that day.

On a full stomach, Manny looked for a place to rest. A small ailanthus tree, whose trunk had broken off in its early life, had a profusion of new branches fighting to become the lead trunk. Some dried leaves were caught in the cradle where the branches diverged. It was a perfect nest.

When he awoke, the sun was near enough to rising that light was sliding in among the trees, revealing a large shadow approaching from the west—and beside it, another, smaller one. The bears. Manny ran toward the rising sun.

As much as Manny liked to run, he did not feel like doing it right now. It seemed like the grove of mostly ailanthus trees was endless, and he wondered if he would ever get back to the woodpile. From his flight with the hawk, he remembered a pasture with a lake just beyond these trees, and that was his goal of the moment.

He ran in the heavy shadows of the dense tree canopy until the east-facing branches of the trees began stretching broadly toward the light of an open field. There was a fence defining the beginnings of a pasture with open grass to the east. Manny scrambled to the top of a locust fence-post to look around. Just ahead and slightly to the south, the land tapered away to a sizable lake—the one he had seen from the sky.

Manny's thought was to eat some of the seeds from pokeweeds growing next to the lake and find a place to sleep until dark. He would begin crossing the pasture at night. As he approached the lake's edge just north of two large boulders, he heard the sound. It wasn't loud. It was a plaintive, pleading call to the primal forces of creation to restructure nature with mercy and freedom for all. The call rippled a dirge of fear and death across the airwaves, a hopeless, helpless call.

Manny knew what it was. A snake had a small animal in its stare, maybe a mouse, though the tone was a bit wrong for a mouse. The sound was coming from the other side of the boulders where he saw what he feared he would. A large blacksnake had an animal in its stare. It was Gophericious.

Only a short distance separated Gophericious from the snake. There was little time. Still, initially, Manny watched, unable to move. The snake was not staring at him, but he could not help staring at it. His friend's cry stopped his heart and locked down his muscles. Manny watched the snake's tongue flick, watched its unblinking eyes burn their fatal glare. But the eyes were not on him. It was he who was staring at the snake. He was in control. He bolted forward, running straight toward the snake. "Run, Gophericious, run," he yelled as he broke the plane between the snake and his friend.

The spell was broken. Gophericious darted behind Manny and to his side. The snake turned to catch their eyes, but there was no chance. Manny and Gophericious ran as fast as Manny could go, and they did not look back. They circled past the boulders and out into the pasture. Well away from the snake, they stopped.

"I sure am glad to see you. What on earth brought you out here? You're a long way from home, you know. Your name is Manny, right? I don't forget names—or faces for that matter. My real name is Gophericious, Godominic, Gopherberg, Gopherian, Gophersky, Gopherov, Gopherson. But you can just call me Go. Everybody does, because go is pretty much all I do. I come from a long line of gophers that roamed these fields back when there were dinosaurs here. Did I tell you all this the first time we met? Just interrupt me if I did. I get on a roll, and I don't know how to stop."

"It's all right. I'm just glad to see you. I've been away from home; it's great to see someone I know. Can you show me how to get home?"

"Well, the direction is easy. You just head toward the sun when it comes up in the morning and run away from it when it's setting in the evening. Eventually, you'll get there, but I have to tell you, it's a very long way from here at the speed you run. Even for me, this is a long trip. I've never been this far before. I kinda got a little too much go in me today. I was goin' and goin' and goin', you know, just on the go, so to speak. Next thing I knew, I was way beyond anywhere I'd been before. It's getting dark. Even at my speed, I can't get home tonight. I don't know where to go."

"Come with me. The fence back that way is overgrown with multiflora rose bushes, poison ivy, and honeysuckle. It'll be perfect."

The strange friends threaded through the tall grass, Manny running as fast as he could and Gophericious moving at a fast walk. It was hard for Gophericious to move so slowly. When they reached the multiflora, Manny went inside, forgetting that it was not as easy for his friend, who was considerably bigger.

"Ouch. Ooo. Ouch. Oh. Ahh," said Gophericious, squeezing through after Manny. "This may be a safe place, but it's not so easy for something as big as me to get in here. Ouch, ooo, ahh, ay! My body is nothing but scratches and punctures." Gophericious reached the center of the multiflora rose bush where Manny was fixing a nest for them with dried leaves. As soon as he'd settled in, Gophericious launched into his ethnic history. He fell asleep in the middle of a sentence about dinosaurs.

"Excuse me, do you mind if I come in?" whispered a small voice from just outside the innermost part of the rose bush. It sounded and smelled like a mouse.

"Please, come right in. My name's Manny."

"My name is Maia. My family's nest was destroyed, and I have nowhere to go. I saw you save the gopher and followed you. I just need a place to hide until I can figure out what to do next." Maia's feet were white, as though she wore spats, and her eyes had the dancing quality of Manny's mother's eyes. "You were unbelievably brave saving the gopher. Do you know him?"

"Yes, his name's Gophericious, but wait 'till you hear his whole lineage, which I'm sure you will when he wakes up. What happened to your family's nest?"

"Our nest was in a rock wall fence. Yesterday morning a man with a machine came and dug up the rocks. We barely escaped and everyone scattered because of the man's two dogs. I was hiding near the boulders at the lake's edge when I heard your friend, Gopheriscut?"

"Gophericious."

"Yes, anyway, I watched what happened. I hope you don't mind that I followed you. Your scent was easy to follow. You smell good," she said, before she realized what she'd said and turned away in embarrassment. "I mean as a mouse, as opposed to another animal. Mice smell good, don't you think?"

"Yes, we do," said Manny, searching for a response that would get him past feeling overwhelmed by Maia's sudden presence in his world. "Especially field mice, because we eat good food. Have you ever been around house mice? They smell different. It's their diet."

Manny could tell from the look on Maia's face that she did not know what he was talking about, and he thought he must have messed up somehow. He searched her face for reassurance that she was not offended. Maia was the prettiest name he'd ever heard, and she was the warmest and softest looking, most beautiful mouse he had ever seen. She smelled good too, of course, but he did not say that. "You can sleep without worry here. You're among friends."

"I don't want to be any trouble. I'm afraid I don't know as much as you do," Maia said, looking at the ground.

"I'm sure you know things I don't. I still have a lot to learn."

"I have to find my family, but I'd like to spend more time... I mean... I'm afraid... I mean, if I can't find my family, will you help me find a safe place for a nest?" Maia stopped. She was embarrassed to be asking Manny for help. She was embarrassed most of all that he might know she did not want him to leave.

"I'm searching for my family's nest too, but I have plenty of time. My journey is long. I'd be glad to help you," Manny said, hardly recognizing himself in the words. Why would he interrupt his journey home, the journey that was the sole focus of his life, to help this mouse he'd only just met?

"That would be wonderful. I'm worried about my family, but I'm also afraid of being alone. I don't think I'm ready for that."

"Probably, nobody ever feels ready."

"But you're on your own, aren't you? How did you end up far from your home?"

"I'm embarrassed to tell you. I was careless, lucky to be alive, really. I got distracted for just a minute. That's all it takes."

"What happened?"

Manny told her the story.

"That's incredible. If I were in the talons of a hawk, I think I would just close my eyes and prepare for death."

"You might surprise yourself. Your instinct would be to fight, to do whatever you could to escape," said Manny looking at Maia, seeing her looking at him, sensing that everything was about to change, wanting to take charge, feeling unsure of what to do. "You look tired," he said to buy time. "I know I am. We can talk more tomorrow."

Manny did not sleep well. He lay awake thinking about Maia. He felt she was special without understanding why. And she had said he was brave. Though he knew that breaking the snake's spell was not magic, he wished it were. If it were magic, it would mean he had become Zeus, an invincible mouse. He drifted off, thinking about the truly magical things that would be possible if he were Zeus.

* * *

He dreamed of a splendid mouse palace with hand-made, Turkish wool carpets covering every inch of floor so that when you stepped into the palace, the rich texture of their designs would flood you with the honor of being in the presence of Zeus. Thin, silk Persian carpets covered the walls and the divans for guests to sit in the receiving room. Unlike a real mouse nest, this palace had a large opening through which all creatures could pass, even exceptionally large animals like elephants, because Zeus did not have to hide. Zeus feared no beast or fowl.

The reception hall was a busy place. Animals of every kind came to seek his counsel, to have their disputes settled, and to seek his blessing on their endeavors. Zeus sat on one of the finest of the silk carpets draped over a leather ottoman and rested against a finely embroidered pillow.

The omnivorous guests were served tea, fruit, cookies, and a variety of grasses and vegetables. Carnivores were served tofu heavily doused with poultry spice. It tasted exactly like chicken, and no one seemed to notice it wasn't real chicken. Zeus was careful that it was not served to any of the chickens who came to visit. Fortunately, chickens, though fond of meat, are omnivores and always quite pleased with the fruit and cookies—delicacies they were not often served on their farms.

In fact, chickens didn't come often. They don't take to reasoning well. Zeus's guidance required reasoning powers to make any sense. He believed in empowering the animals who came to him with solutions that they could use again and again, if they understood them. Unfortunately, animals can be lazy. Sometimes Zeus became frustrated that they wanted him to solve their problems for them.

On this particular day, the receiving parlor was filled with an eclectic assortment of birds and animals. There was a pig, a chipmunk, a parrot, a kangaroo, a tiger, a finch, a bat, a rhinoceros, a blue jay, and a cat.

Zeus listened to each of them, though more intently to some than to others. He suspected that the pig, who complained about a sensitive stomach and the indignity of being fed garbage, really only came to eat. He came almost every day and ate a lot, even when he complained that his stomach was bothering him. Also, he had a guilty look on his face.

Zeus was also tired of listening to the blue jay. He couldn't remember what specifically the blue jay was complaining about today. It didn't seem to be life-threatening or painful. He felt a little bad that he couldn't remember what the blue jay had said. Unfortunately, that would mean he'd have to raise the subject again but in a way that wouldn't make it obvious he'd not been listening the first time.

Zeus prided himself on being a good listener and vowed not to be distracted even by the harsh tones of the blue jay. It was possible that the blue jay faced some genuine distress, instead of causing distress to others, which was normally what happened. In the background, a parrot was quietly making fun of the blue jay by imitating it in a low whisper to the delight of the other guests. Zeus considered putting a stop to it, but decided it was harmless.

The tiger's problem was easy. He had a thorn in his foot, and Zeus was able to remove it quickly. As soon as it came out, the tiger's pain was gone, and he started to lick the wound. He was also hungry and looked at Zeus for a moment, but Zeus directed such a glare at him that he felt terrible and immediately reached for a cookie and a piece of tofu. The taste of chicken was quite satisfying.

The rhinoceros had a huge problem. His habitat had been gradually settled by farmers who drove him out, and he had nowhere to live. "I need a lot of space," he explained. "I need a place with many plants to eat and water for drinking, bathing, and keeping cool. I have a cousin who went to a zoo, but I don't know how to get there, and I'd prefer to stay somewhere in the wild, I think."

Zeus assured him that he would transport him to a place where rhinoceroses were protected, if he could just wait while he attended to a few other animals' problems first.

A chipmunk told a frightening tale of getting chased by a feral cat and how, after narrowly escaping death, the chipmunk had found himself disoriented with no idea as to where his home and his wife and children were.

* * *

In the middle of this tale, Manny awoke, feeling overwhelmed at his own predicament. He was not lost. He knew he was going in the right direction. But now he had promised to help Maia, as well. He wasn't sure how he felt about that. *Would he feel better if he had only himself to think about? Why did he agree to help her? Wasn't he in enough trouble without taking on someone else's problems?* Manny's thoughts were interrupted by Gophericious, who stirred and jumped to his feet.

"Well, good morning, Manny. Ouch, I forgot we're surrounded by thorns. I dare say, I'm happy that we spent the night safely, but I don't think I would ever again choose to enter the inner sanctum of these mutliflora rose bushes. Most inhospitable. A gopher could get fatally stabbed just rolling over too quickly in the midst of a bad dream. And who are you?" he asked, turning toward Maia, whom he had awakened with his chatter.

"My name's Maia."

"Beautiful name. My goodness, and I have been so rude not introducing myself. My name's Gophericious. Well my full name is Gophericious, Godominic, Gopherberg, Gopherian, Gophersky, Gopherov, Gopherson. But you can just call me Go. Everybody does, because go is pretty much all I do. If I had time, I'd explain our connection to dinosaurs, but I need to get back on the road, get on the go, if you know what I mean. Go, go, go, that's the agenda for today. I plan to head right toward that morning sun and keep going 'till its last rays warm my back. I'd travel with you, Manny, if I could, but I just can't run slow."

"Don't worry about me. I'll get home. And I want to stay and help Maia first anyway."

"All right then. I need to push off. You two be careful. But who am I talking to. I guess you know as much about staying alive as I do. Mostly I don't slow down, hoping to be out of sight before any creature can contemplate my demise. Hasta la vista, baby!"

The cold breeze that blew as Manny and Maia stepped out from under the multiflora felt incongruous with the bright sun, which seemed powerless in this early morning to wring the earth's surface of cold and moisture. "It's cold," said Maia. "We need to eat. There's a clump of persimmon trees down the fence-line."

Two deer were eating persimmons, but paid them no attention. Manny smelled bear poop, but didn't say anything. If there were a bear nearby, the deer would have been frightened off. Still, Manny felt the bear's recent presence was not a good sign.

"I see my sister, Tanya, coming." said Maia. "Tanya, over here! Manny, this is my sister. Tanya, this is Manny. Have you seen any of the rest of the family?"

"Nice to meet you, Manny. No, you're the first. We should go back to our rock wall. Everyone will go back there."

The smell of newly disturbed earth greeted them before they reached the scar in the land where part of the rock wall had been removed. "Look, there's Mother," said Maia, pointing to a mouse waving from the top of the rocks. Her mother had a tuft of white hair on her neck that she blamed on a narrow escape from a feral cat.

"Mom, Mom," yelled Maia and Tanya, as they approached. They hugged and danced in a circle.

"I raised a couple of smart girls," their mother, Linda, said, hugging them once more, but looking anxiously across the field. "I hope Gloria, Jim, and Gary find their way here soon," she added, referring to her other children.

"They're probably hiding, waiting to be sure it's safe to return," said Tanya.

"They'll come back here, mother, just like we did. This is home." said Maia. "I want you to meet my new friend. Mother, this is Manny."

Maia told her mother and sister how she had met Manny and how Manny happened to be in their pasture. Manny shifted his weight from one side to the other unsure of what to say, what to do, what to expect, or how to continue on his way home. Change was happening too fast.

"I'm happy to meet you," he managed to say, spared from anything more by the sudden burst of noise that turned their heads to the far end of the pasture. The airwaves were pounding, undulating with the roar of a tractor and punctured by the noise of yelping dogs.

"They're coming back," said Linda. "Quick, your father has been gathering grass for a new nest farther down the rock wall."

They ran along the base of the rock wall with the noise of the machine and the dogs pressing in on them. The noise marched relentless and pounded their eardrums. Robert, Maia's father, arrived at the spot at almost the same moment, and all of them squirmed through the narrow passages that led to the nest under construction inside.

"Dad, this is Manny," said Maia. "He helped me find cover last night and came with me to help me find you and Mom."

"Pleased to meet you, young man," said Robert. "Unfortunately, these are not propitious circumstances."

For a long time, everyone just sat quiet. It was hard to talk anyway, because of the noise. The tractor's engine growled as though angry at the peace and quiet of the pasture, angry at the rocks, angry at the dogs, angry at the huddled mice in the wall.

19. The Long March

Dal came over to sniff at the entrance to their nest, bringing a wave of dog breath into the chamber where they were hiding.

"What's that you're smellin', Dal?" came the voice of Farmer Frank over the roar of the tractor. Manny could hear the dog at the entrance to their hole, scratching at the rocks and whining.

"Found something, have you? Probably nothing more than a mouse. What if there's a copperhead in there? Your nose is too busy, that's all."

Manny heard Farmer Frank walk right up to where they had entered the rock wall, and now he could smell the tobacco. Farmer Frank started to move some of the rocks for Dal. Manny thought that Farmer Frank might be angry if he remembered the refrigerator. "If we get exposed, everyone run in different directions," he said, but whispered, "Follow me," to Maia.

Farmer Frank gave a grunt as he moved a particularly large rock. "There'd better be something interesting in here," he said just as a rock tumbled down, grazing the fingers on his left hand and landing square on his big toe.

"Ahhh!" he screamed, along with a few other things. Dal moved to establish a little more distance between himself and Farmer Frank, who did not seem in the kind of mood that would inspire a dog to present himself as man's best friend.

"Stupid mutt," Farmer Frank said after he'd stopped jumping around. He got back on the tractor and began scooping up the rocks, filling the trailer before he reached the part of the wall where Manny and his new friends were hiding.

Inside the wall, Maia's father, Robert, finally said, "Our ancestors have lived in this wall as far back as stories are told. My grandfather's grandfather had a nest in this wall. It fits here; it belongs here."

Maia's mother, Linda, broke the silence. "Robert, you scout a new place to build a nest. I'll wait here. Gary, Jim, and Gloria will look for us here."

"Farther down the fence, there's another section of rock wall that Tanya and I found one day," said Maia. "It's mostly fallen down and overgrown with vines. It would make a great place for a nest."

"You can lead us there," answered her father.

"Tanya can show you. I want to help Manny find *his* family. I would like your and Mother's blessing to go with Manny." Maia surprised even herself in how she blurted this out. She moved to hug her mother, so that each of them would have space to digest what she had said.

"I know it's time for you to leave home," her mother responded slowly and carefully. "I know you are grown and that your sisters and brothers, too, will be leaving soon. But I always imagined you would leave with one of our neighbors' children and live near us—in the same rock wall." She held onto Maia, tightly, lovingly.

"So did I. But this feels like the right thing to do. You taught me so much, Mother. I feel I'm ready to go," Maia said, gently pulling away just enough to look her mother in the eyes and let her smiling and confident expression show that she loved her mother—and that she was ready to leave.

"Well, we never know the future. If you want to help Manny find his home, you may do so. Maia is well prepared, Manny. You may be surprised at all she knows. If you would like Maia to travel with you, she has our blessing; isn't that right, Robert?"

"I guess so. It's just kind of sudden. We hardly know this young mouse."

"He protected me the first night after our nest was destroyed. And he saved the life of a gopher," Maia said to emphasize that she had chosen wisely.

Her father responded by moving to her side and giving her a hug. "Your mother is right. You have our prayers for a safe journey."

"Here comes Gary," yelled Tanya.

Gary was puffing hard. He had obviously run a long distance. "Am I glad to see you," he said. "Gloria and Jim are waiting at the section of rock wall down the fence-line. There are many good places for nests there."

"Let's get started," said Linda.

"How do we know Farmer Frank won't come for the rocks in that wall?" asked Robert. "He seems determined to dig up every rock wall there is."

"Well, how many rocks can he need?" asked Linda. "The sun is setting. Maia, come, give us each one last hug. You need to be off, and so do we."

"Give my love to Gloria and Jim," Maia said.

* * *

Manny set a slow pace that caused minimal disturbance to the tall grass in the unmowed and ungrazed pasture. They could see almost nothing and also could not easily be seen. "We'll keep moving through the night," Manny said. "Or at least until we come to a good hiding place to spend the day."

"I know this pasture. We can hide in the small groundhog city that's up ahead. It's overgrown with partridge berry, pokeweed, spice bushes, and vines of every kind. We should be able to see it from that rock," Maia said, pointing to a rock that rose above the grass a short distance ahead.

Little light was left as they climbed to the top of the rock, but the sky was still a gray slate that displayed the silhouettes of every flying creature. They were watching two small birds circle hurriedly nearby when a wedge of a hundred honking geese broke the northern horizon.

Manny shuddered, remembering his encounter with the hawk. The wingspan of the approaching birds was frightening, and their strident honks seemed to foretell a nasty disposition. "Quick," he yelled. "Get back down in the grass before those birds see us."

"Those are geese," said Maia. "They started coming a few days ago. Father says they come twice in the cycle of the seasons. They'll land in the lake for the night and leave in the morning."

"Are you sure they're safe? The sky's full of them."

"They only eat seeds. They're highly organized. They post sentries and take turns watching for danger."

"They fly different from other birds."

"They take turns in the lead to break the wind for each other. If you get tired, I will break the grass for you. Together, we'll make it, just like the geese."

A full moon broke golden in the east. Instead of darkness, a white light revealed every detail on earth. They sat on the rock—two small mice—under a sky too big to see them, but too small to hide them.

Resuming their journey, Manny ran faster now, and Maia surprised him. He almost had to run at full speed to keep ahead of her. He felt his muscles pushing hard to set the pace. It felt great, and the smell of berries, weed seeds, and groundhogs increasingly overpowered that of the grass through which they ran, giving them a burst of energy to the edge of the groundhog city where the grass stopped and the weeds, vines, and brush began.

Maia stepped forward onto one of the groundhog trails into what appeared an impenetrable wall of darkness. "This way," she said, pointing to the other side of the trail, "I smell partridge berries and spicebush seeds."

Manny followed, knowing he would not have stepped into the blackness so quickly if he'd been alone.

They ate in silence and settled into a pile of leaves. "How many days do you think we are from the woodpile?" asked Maia.

"I wish I knew. We may be many days away. Maybe you should rejoin your family. If something happens to you, it would be my fault."

"No, it wouldn't. This was my choice. We'll make it. I feel safe."

Maia closed her eyes, pressed against him, and drifted into sleep. Manny lay listening to her easy breathing. He wished he were as confident as Maia. He had expected to be traveling alone. Now, there was Maia. Manny fell asleep worrying that he needed a plan and dreamed of Zeus.

* * *

Every square foot of Zeus's palace carpeting was taken up by animals in some degree of real or imagined distress. A group of foxes was staging a protest, carrying signs that declared them to be on a hunger strike and demanding that Zeus lift the prohibition on eating mice. Zeus rolled his eyes. Did they really expect anyone to believe they were on a hunger strike?

The apparent leader led them in chanting, "We want mice; we want mice. Mice for the masses, mice for the stew, mice for your children, and mice for you!"

Their spokesfox read a statement. "Honorable Zeus, Sir, we wish to call to your attention the impracticality of your ban on eating mice. We humbly suggest that you have not considered the consequences of your action. What will happen to us if you protect all the mice from harm? We are not vegetarians. We demand equal consideration in this kingdom. What are we supposed to eat?" she asked, looking menacingly around the room. Several ground hogs shifted uncomfortably and a rat ducked down behind a pig. "Half our families are so thin," continued the spokesfox, "they look like boney cats."

A tiger growled low and looked at the spokesfox, who quickly blurted, "I didn't mean regal-looking cats like you, Mr. Tiger; I meant those flea-bitten, ugly little things that scamper around abandoned barns and fields. Surely, you're not related to those beasts? I ate one once. It looked all fat and juicy, but by the time I got through the hair, there was nothing but bones and gristle. Spoiled my appetite for a week."

"Have you tried fish?" asked Zeus, more out of a sense of frustration than a conviction that fish should be eaten.

"Fish?" asked the spokesfox. "No, I hadn't thought of becoming a fish-eater. I've seen bears catch fish and eat them, but I don't think I'm well equipped for that. Have you smelled a bear's breath? No other fox would come near you. Anyway, bears have foul tempers and are generally disagreeable, nasty creatures, I ..."

The spokesfox was cut off mid-sentence by a bear who roared and stepped forward. All the foxes took a step back in unison, but Zeus stepped between the bear and the foxes to calm the situation.

This provided the opening the hawks had been looking for. They picked up the chant of the foxes. "We want mice. We want mice. Mice for the masses, mice for the stew, mice for your children, and mice for you!" Zeus again rolled his eyes. It just confirmed what he'd always heard about birds—not too big in the brain department. They couldn't even come up with their own chant.

Meanwhile the spokescat for the house-cats in attendance had been sharpening his claws on one of Zeus's better silk carpets while waiting for his opportunity to speak, pushing Zeus to the limits of his patience.

The spokescat was a large Persian with immaculately brushed, shiny black hair and just one small distinguishing spot of white over his right eye, giving him a kind of pirate look. The cat cleared his throat with excessive pomp and leaped gracefully to the top of the table where he quickly popped a chicken-flavored tofu hors d'oeuvre in his mouth, cleared his throat once again, and addressed the group while casting a disdainful glance at the foxes.

"Friends, neighbors, fellow sojourners on this bountiful earth," he began. Turning to the foxes, he continued, "On behalf of the mice-eaters of the world—and here I include in my appeal even the unworthy foxes among us whose earlier remarks simply put an exclamation point on their base nature—I have to note that most mice-eaters are not driven by malice, but hunger, and do not select mice randomly but purposefully as the select crème de la crème of edibles. It's more a quality of life issue than one of survival. Surely mice wish to contribute to the quality of life on earth? Speaking for cats, as I do, I can say that quality of life is a paramount concern of ours—not just for ourselves, of course, but for all creatures. To each some joy and a little sacrifice. It seems only fair."

Zeus looked at the cat, not hiding his disgust. This guy obviously ate prepared cat food and hunted nothing out of hunger. Zeus had a terrible headache. The idea of protecting all mice had seemed a goal of innate merit devoid of negative consequences. How could there be anything wrong with keeping mice from being eaten? But it was proving to be a goal that demanded much of Zeus in its achievement. He felt physically and emotionally exhausted.

20. The Bears

Manny and Maia slept through most of the day. After eating more seeds and berries, they slipped out from under the heavy brush into the fading sunlight. It offered little warmth. They pushed through the tall grass, walking, running, and stopping to look, to listen, and to turn their noses to the wind. Night carried in the dew without moving, placed it silently, and beaded every blade of grass. Manny and Maia were soon soaked and cold.

"Let's stop here," Maia said, pointing to a flat rock that broke the plane of the grass. "The rock will have retained some heat from the daytime sun."

Manny shivered, his cold, wet body grateful they had stopped. The rock felt warm. If he had been by himself, he would have kept moving. But maybe this was the better thing to be doing.

"It's not how fast we get there, but how safe," said Maia, as though reading his mind. "We won't rest any longer than we need to."

Their wet bodies sent steam rising to greet a gentle south breeze that promised warmth in the morning. Tempting as it was to stay on the rock for the rest of the night, they soon continued toward the trees of a fence-line on the eastern horizon where they arrived just before dawn. They had crossed the pasture. The tree-line they reached separated the pasture from the hay field. Several of the trees were dogwoods with plentiful berries. After they'd eaten, Maia pointed to one of the trees. "We'll be safe in that tree."

"Why that one?"

"It has a built-in sentry. See the turtle dove's nest? If an animal comes, the turtle dove will hear it. When they hear or see anything coming, they flutter to the ground and run, flapping their wings awkwardly, as though too injured to fly. They trick the predator, moving away just as fast as necessary to keep ahead of them, luring them far from their nest. We can sleep in this tree without a worry."

Deep in the rock wall fence or the woodpile of their parents' nests they would not have slept more soundly. The walk had been exhausting, their bed of leaves in a hollow crevice was comfortable, and the unseasonable southern breeze helped keep them warm.

They were astonished to find that most of the day had passed before they awoke. The second surprise was the ground. Just beyond where they'd eaten the dogwood berries were walnuts for a hearty breakfast. And once again there was bear poop. Maia looked at Manny, as if to ask what he thought.

"The bears are no threat to us. They have plenty to eat," Manny said, trying to reassure himself as much as Maia. "The woodpile should be that way." Manny pointed away from where the sun was completing its path across the sky. The last light of a clear day waited for them to eat.

Manny saw the cub first. It was eating nuts a few trees south of where they were. He motioned to Maia to hold still. The cub, small and black, was intent in its eating, picking up each nut and chewing at the shell until it broke open to reveal the nut-meat inside. It would have continued unaware of them or anything else, except for the bark of the dog. Dal appeared.

The cub looked at Dal, unafraid and not particularly interested. Dal looked at the cub and saw an animal perfect for chasing. He barked and moved toward the cub to provoke it to run. The cub growled but more as a call to its mother than as a challenge to Dal. Dal did not make the distinction. He heard the growl as a show of bravado. He barked more loudly and advanced closer.

Manny and Maia watched—an audience to this play without fear for themselves—watched to see from where the mother bear would come. She would come. She would come angry, protective, and intent on death to Dal.

Roooaaar!! Roooaaar!! The sound terrified Dal's wagging tail stiff, his joints motionless, his eyes uneager, as the mother bear burst from the trees. Dal, despite the fear that dominated his body, did not turn away. His adrenaline was pumping. He barked loudly, trying to assert control, but he moved unsure and defensively in a half-circle facing the bear.

The cub, content to let its mother take over, moved slightly away and closer to Manny and Maia, who did not move. The smells of fear, of dog, of bears covered the earth, and yet Maia's nose picked up the smell of concentrated sweetness. In the small pine tree next to where the cub now waited, she also heard bees, stirred by the noise of the dog and the bear, circling their home, their queen, their treasure of honey.

In what was likely to be a life and death contest for Dal, Manny felt pulled to Dal. Never mind that he was a young, stupid dog who never should have barked at the cub. Dal had once saved his life. Dal was familiar. He was part of the world of Farmer Frank's farm to which Manny intended to return, and he wanted to find it the way he had left it, including Dal. Who knew what kind of dog Farmer Frank might replace Dal with, if Dal got himself killed? Manny ran toward the space between the mother bear and Dal.

Maia yelled for him to stop, but he didn't. So she turned and ran directly at the cub, executing her own plan. The cub was watching its mother and Dal. Maia knew it wouldn't see her unless she almost ran into it, and she did. She ran right over the cub's right front paw and up the pine tree.

The cub, startled, did not react instantly. It looked down at its paw and then at the mouse running up the tree, raising its nose right to the honey—which was definitely more interesting than the sparring match between its mother and a dog. It also forgot all about Maia who had moved around to the back side of the tree-trunk and was coming back down, hidden from view. The cub bounded up the tree, totally focused on the sweet reward of a bee hive.

Meanwhile, Dal faced the enemy. The bear was big and smelled of danger. Dal growled low and barked, baring his teeth, a strategy that worked in most situations, making the attacker think twice about confrontation—but not a mother bear who thinks her cub is under threat. She rose up on her back legs, preparing to lunge at Dal with her razor-sharp claws, preparing to bring the wrath of nature's law down in judgment on this violator.

Manny saw Dal about to get slashed, yet ran toward the impending blood-bath with no fear; he ran as Zeus, Lord of Lightning, Titan of Thunder. "Run, Dal, run!" he yelled.

Manny's appearance on the battlefield distracted the fighters. Dal spun to the right. The bear cast a glance toward Manny mid-motion, disrupting her timing and slowing the speed of her paw's descent on Dal. The claws that otherwise would have ripped fatally into Dal's body tore only through his right hind leg just above the knee, tearing muscle and tendons, exposing the bone.

Dal fell to the ground and let out a horrified yelp of pain. Followed by another and another. The bear paused, watching Dal on the ground moaning, whimpering. Then she rose up, roared again and exposed her claws for another blow. Dal cowered, yelped, and tried to move. Manny watched, unable to help.

A crashing noise and a scream from her cub held the mother bear on her hind legs and turned her head back toward the pine tree from where her cub's scream had come. The small pine had snapped from the cub's weight, sending the bee hive and the cub falling with a swarm of angry bees in pursuit. The mother bear loped to her cub, who picked himself up, unhurt. Mother and cub attacked the honey as the bees discharged their stings on hair and skin too tough to feel them.

21. Bonding

"Dal," said Manny. "Are you all right? We need to get out of here."

"I don't think I can move. My hip is on fire, and my leg won't move. Anyway, who are you?" Dal intently licked the deep gash in his right hind leg, holding the bleeding in check mostly, though blood trickled onto the ground.

"I'll tell you later. Right now, you need to move, even if only a little bit. The bear needs to see that our intent is to leave."

Dal made a feeble effort to rise, yelping, moaning, and whining as he did so.

"Try getting up on your front legs," said Maia, who had joined them. "Then pull up your rear with the leg that's not hurt."

"I can't put any weight on my legs. The pain is terrible," Dal said, whincing and letting out an extended whimper.

"That's your wounded leg. The other legs only feel as though they'll hurt if you put weight on them, but they won't."

Dal curled his front legs under him and whimpered as he pushed himself up.

"That's great," said Maia. "Now pull your good rear leg tight up under you and lift up."

Dal sat up with his front legs straight, though shaking. Then he pushed up on his left hind leg and stood wobbling on three legs with the right rear one hanging loose beside him. He was whimpering but standing. Manny and Maia let out a cheer: "Hurray! Way to go!"

Manny looked over where the bears appeared to be finishing off the honey. The next few minutes would decide their fate. "Okay," he said. "Now take small steps with your front legs and small jumps with your good rear leg, so the bear sees you intend to leave."

"I can't," said Dal. "I have to sit back down."

"Just hop for a few steps. Then you can rest," said Manny.

Dal stood immobile on three legs as time raced ahead, uncaring. Manny looked back at the bears. The mother bear stood facing in their direction, watching, undecided. *Maybe the sweet of the honey will calm her, make her less angry*, Manny hoped. Dal stood wavering, unsure, self-pitying, and smelling of blood, of fear.

"Dal, your life depends on it," said Maia. "Take one step. Just one."

And he did. Dal took a small step with his front legs and brought his rear along with a short hop off his good rear leg. He panted a deep sigh of relief and pride and took a second step. "Okay," he said. "I can do this. Mind you, the pain is horrific. I wouldn't be able to do it if I were without a pedigree."

Manny watched the mother bear. She was playing with her cub, content with a stomach full of honey and a vanquished enemy.

Dal moved a hop at a time, resting after each jump. He whimpered, but a little less so each time. "You didn't tell me who you are. I think I owe you my life," he said to Manny.

"What saved both of us was the cub falling out of the pine tree, however that happened."

"I smelled the honey," said Maia. "I didn't know if it would work, but it was the only thing I could think to do."

"You still didn't tell me who you are, and how you know me?" said Dal.

"I know you from Farmer Frank's garden. My name's Manny and this is my friend Maia. You chased me and my friend, a rabbit, one night in the garden, and you saved me from a snake once."

"I've killed a few snakes. Glad it was helpful. If I chased you and a rabbit in the garden, though, I don't understand how you got away. I catch everything that comes in there."

"I guess that was one of your off nights. We should keep moving."

Once he got the hang of hopping, Dal could make faster time than Manny and Maia could run, so he let them run up his tail onto his back. The hopping made it hard for them to hold on, but it was great to cover ground with no fear of predators. Dal stopped frequently to lick his wound and stop the bleeding.

They spent the rest of the day crossing the hay field that Manny remembered from when he was flying in the talons of the hawk. After this field, only the corn field lay between them and home. It was dark when they reached the round hay bales stacked along the fence that separated the hay field from the corn field, the last field between them and the woodpile.

Excess straw from bales of successive years made a perfect bed for Dal's tired body. He curled against one of the bales out of the wind and began licking his wound, keenly aware of the pain, the throbbing, the burning. He willed himself to sleep, hoping to awake from a bad dream and find himself running in the garden on the heels of a rabbit, running in the pasture on the trail of too many scents to decide which one to follow.

Manny and Maia crawled into a crevice between two hay bales behind Dal's back where they had protection from all sides and heat from Dal's body. As they settled in, Maia started humming softly, "Would you mind if I sing a song? I love to sing, especially when I'm feeling good or when I need to slow down my thoughts to understand what I'm feeling. Singing helps me."

"Is it all right if I listen?"

"Of course. I want you to. I'll be singing to myself, but I'd love it if you wanted to hear me. The words may seem sad, but I won't be feeling sad. It's hard to explain. It's just the way the music is."

I've got the field mouse blues,
Blues is what I've got 'em.

When you're at the bottom,
You've got the food chain blues.
The fox wants to eat,
The cat wants to play.
If I keep my wits,
I survive today.
I've got the field mouse blues,
Blues is what I've got `em.
When you're at the bottom,
You've got the food chain blues.

"I've never heard a sound so beautiful. Where did you learn to sing like that?"

"Thank you. I learned from an uncle of mine who disappeared. He sang to me every night, and I sang with him. Singing made me less afraid even when the songs were about things we need to fear. Music is healing, my uncle said, because songs never leave us. They're always there, ready to pop back in our heads, like spirits."

They lay in silence, listening to their beating hearts, soaking in warmth, watching darkness, gathering thoughts they were afraid to speak. The moon quickened its pace across the sky with stringy clouds playing hide and seek with its face, and Maia was soon asleep.

Manny lay awake afraid to blink, lest his eyelids stay closed, lest he awake unable to hear Maia's song in his head. Everything that preceded Maia seemed a long time ago and detached from him. *Was it he who had escaped the hawk, who had followed the rivulets of rainwater down, down, down the trunk of the tree amid the fire and tympani, who had slid into the water on the beaver's back and surfaced as captain of the ship?*

Even Farmer Frank's farm seemed more a fantasy than the world of Zeus. When he left the woodpile but a few days before, he was searching for a presence he knew only in its absence. But now, Maia was asleep beside him, and whatever he would do the next day, would be with her.

Only three days before, he had been alone, wondering whether it made sense to try to get home. But tomorrow, he would go home so that Dal would go home; he would go home to give Maia a home. And he was not afraid. Tomorrow, he and Maia would confront life together. Manny exhaled a deep sigh of contentment and was soon asleep, dreaming of Zeus and of Zeus's new partner, Athena.

* * *

Outwardly, the palace was as always. The Turkish and Persian carpets were in place, including the carpet that showed the effects of the Persian cat's clawing of it. But rebellion was afoot. The usual mouse-eaters were not seeking help or council but bore petitions, seeking waivers from the regulations that banned the eating of mice in Zeus's kingdom. Zeus did not feel like listening to this nonsense.

"Sir," began a great horned owl perched high on the crystal chandelier, "known, as I am among creatures, for my wisdom, scholarship, deductive logic, and intuitive thinking, I have been elected to present a proposal which I know you will find unassailable in its reasoning, logic, good sense, and fairness to all. What we propose is a hunting season—actually several hunting seasons."

"A hunting season? What kind of hunting season? What's to be hunted?"

"Well, er, ah, I mean. . . we thought. . . that is, we propose. . . . Well, you know, many of us here do hunt mice, so. . ."

"You want official sanction to hunt mice? That's absurd."

"Just hear me out, if you would, please. It's not quite what it sounds. And there are some serious pluses in this for the mice, I dare say."

Zeus did not respond.

"Well, as I was saying," said the great horned owl, continuing with a watchful eye on Zeus's rod, "the proposal actually calls for several hunting seasons. The first would be open only to domestic dogs. They are not at all effective mousers. They are chasers of mice, really. That would be followed by the domestic cat season. Many of them are too lazy to even chase a mouse, but we have to acknowledge that they do have the capacity to cause mice mortal harm. And occasionally they do.

"The next season would be for wild cats. They are extremely dangerous for mice, but there are few of them. Then would come the snakes. There are lots of them, but they don't have large appetites. One mouse a month satisfies most of them. Perhaps you are beginning to see the logic of this proposal. It gives the mice a head start so to speak. They get to practice their survival skills against increasingly more dangerous predators, giving them the maximum chance of survival. That's the fair thing about this proposal, don't you think?"

Zeus said nothing—just stared with part incredulity and part threat in his glare. "Well, then, to continue," said the owl cautiously, "the owls would come next, because we are not abundant, and we hunt mostly at night with the benefit of our exceptional night vision. Then would come the foxes, and finally, the hawks. We believe this proposal represents a fair compromise. It requires all of us to endure some periods of vegetarianism, or, in some cases, meals of larger animals with less tasty flesh who could represent some danger to us in their capture. But we are all willing to share the pain as part of this negotiated settlement.

"And finally, the best part of this proposal—to put a capstone on the ingenious features I've already described—is that all hunters would be required to buy permits from you—a Zeus mouse tax. And you would be permitted to extract additional financial penalties from any predator caught hunting mice out of its season. All of this income would be yours to use as you see fit. We've noticed, for example, that some of your carpets are looking a bit worn."

Zeus hardly knew how to begin. The carpets looking a bit worn? These stupid creatures had no appreciation for the subtle aging of the natural dyes. Of course, everything would be in better shape without the constant traffic from these brigands, but he certainly was not about to replace any of his prized carpets.

As Zeus searched for the right words to respond, a soft, but strong voice came from beside the sofa. "Speaking for mice," the voice said, "we have no desire to be a part of this negotiation. We definitely have no desire to be part of an official hunting season. It is not that we enjoy being hunted at all times by all of you, but rather that we do not want our hunting sanctioned and bought. We will see you in the fields, in the houses, and in the barns. We will wait for you under the haystacks, under the rock fences, and under the woodpiles. On every playing field and battlefield, on every turf and tundra. You will not deplete us. We will match your greed with our abundance, fair and square. No hunting license required. We are not afraid."

All eyes turned to the creature beside the sofa, a sweet-faced mouse with resolute blue eyes, dark gray fur, and white front paws that looked as though she were wearing spats.

"My name is Athena," she continued. "And this negotiation is over. You are on notice. Zeus and I will be everywhere at all times. You may get a mouse now and then, but you'd better get used to broccoli. It's good for you."

22. The Pact

The white quarter moon hung fragile over Dal, Manny, and Maia, offering scant light and no warmth. Even the smallest passing cloud turned it off, so that the cold settled uncontested on the hay bales, on the grass, on the sleeping travelers. Dal shivered involuntarily and Manny awoke. He knew what had to be done. Waking Maia, he said, "I'm going to find my rabbit friend, Rachel. She knows about healing wounds. She can help us get Dal home."

"Dal chases rabbits," said Maia. "I don't think he'd let a rabbit get near him."

"He likes to chase mice, too," said Manny. "His instinct for survival has to trump everything else. He needed us, and now he needs Rachel."

"I'll come with you."

"No, you'd better stay with Dal. If he wakes up, he'll be in a lot of pain and may be disoriented." Manny paused. He looked east toward his destination. It was going to be a long run. He looked at Maia, held by her dancing eyes, locking her look of affection in his mind to carry it with him, to make it the last thing he would see. He nuzzled in close to her and whispered, "I love you."

"Let the stars be your eyes," she said. "Let the clouds be your cart; let the wind be your ears, and your compass my heart. I love you too."

Maia's words filled his head as he crossed the field. He could barely feel the ground under his toes; his muscles got resistance from the earth with each push, but he was not running. He was flying. If his heart was pumping fast, he noticed not. If his muscles tired, he was unaware. If he was hungry, he did not feel it. If he was thirsty, his mouth did not dry.

The hay bales were quickly behind. From the clouded sky, an occasional star checked on his progress, broke the blackness, encouraged this invincible mouse in his flight. The cornfield was no match for Manny. He conquered it without a pause and reached the fence-line where the woodpile and his family's nest lay just to the north. He paused to take in this landmark, the woodpile, the place his mother told him never to leave out of sight, the place he had been unsure he would ever see again. He wanted to tell his mother he was safe, but this was not the time. He continued, instead, to Rachel's warren. "Rachel, Rachel, it's me, Manny. I need your help," he yelled as he descended down the entrance.

"Manny!? I can't see so well in the dark any more. Makes me wonder about all the carrot hype. With all the carrots I've eaten, I should be able to see anything, even in the middle of the night. But I'd recognize your voice anywhere. An old rabbit's eyes might fail, but the ears? Never. They aren't stickin' up there just to make us look beautiful, even if they do."

"I need your help to save Dal. He's been hurt bad. He needs some of your weed paste in the wound."

"Whoa, whoa. What are you talkin' about? You mean Farmer Frank's new dog? What do you have to do with him?"

"I'll tell you as we go. I met this wonderful mouse; her name is Maia."

"Maia? Okay, but what's Maia got to do with that mongrel dog, Dal?"

"I'll explain as we go. I have to get back to Dal and Maia. They're next to the hay bales on the other side of the corn field."

"Okay, I'll come with you. You can ride on my back; we'll make faster time."

"Can we take some of the foam flower with us?"

"We don't need to. Some grows near the hay bales."

Manny rode on her back and recounted his adventure. He told her about the hawk and the beavers and how Maia's family lost its home when Farmer Frank hauled away the rock wall.

"That's interesting," said Rachel. "I've noticed two giant rock ears rising from the ground up by the Franks' house. I guess the rock for them must have come from the rock wall. What about Dal? You still haven't explained how you came to be hanging out with that mongrel and how he got hurt."

Manny told Rachel all the details, except the part about being in love with Maia. He was afraid to mention that in case he would arrive and find it had all been a dream— something he'd imagined, something that had happened to Zeus.

Manny clung to Rachel's back. He would not have asked for it, but he was glad for the ride. In the adrenaline of the night, tired had not reached his brain; now the message was clear. He looked down at Rachel's fur where he was holding onto it. Every hair was white from the root almost to the top. Only because the hair remained its original dark gray color at its very tip, did Rachel still have the appearance of a common rabbit. He could see the original scar and the smaller ones that were left from the owl. Rachel's movement was no longer graceful. The hitch in her hop was pronounced.

Part of Manny wanted to be on the back of a centaur, flying fast across the face of the sky, but mostly, their pace suited him. He had a lot to tell Rachel. He also needed time to think—about Maia, about their future, about a grown-up world without the prospect of becoming Zeus. *Was he ready? And there was Dal. What could he say to Dal that would convince him to let a rabbit put something in his wound? And what about Rachel? How would she behave when she came face to face with Dal?*

Maia saw them coming and ran to meet them. "Rachel, this is Maia," said Manny.

"I'm so pleased to meet you, Rachel," said Maia. "Manny told me you saved his life."

"Yes, I guess I did, but then again, he may have saved my life in the garden too, not to mention from the fox. Manny's a legend in my family. One of my sons saw him fall out of a pokeweed and lure the fox away from our warren." Rachel saw that Manny was embarrassed and changed the subject. "But let me take a look at Dal's wound. We have work to do."

Dal lay on his side with the wounded leg up. The cut seemed to be alive and breathing as Dal's body moved lightly up and down in sleep.

"Nasty slash indeed," said Rachel, surprised that she felt eager to nurse the wound, surprised that Dal looked so helpless. "He'll never use that leg again. I knew a three-legged rabbit once; Rose was her name. She'd taken a shotgun pellet to the lower fibula that snapped it in two. Never could use the leg again for hopping, but she managed pretty well. Lived to see six or seven cycles of the seasons, I think, before…. Well, anyway, let's get to work. I'll get some of the foam flower we need."

Dal began to stir. He whimpered, opened his eyes, raised and twisted his head slightly back toward the wound, and whimpered louder and longer.

"Dal, do you remember me? I'm Manny. We traveled here together after the bear clawed your leg."

Dal whimpered some more and opened his eyes again. "Yes, unfortunately, I remember that this is not just a bad dream. I guess I'll just lie here and starve to death." He whimpered especially loud and long with his eyes closed and indicating no intent to ever raise his head again.

"Look, Dal, it's not that bad. I mean, I know that's easy for me to say ..."

"What he means," interrupted Maia, "is that you should be proud of yourself. You kept your wound clean and the bleeding under control. You may never run as fast as you once did, but you *will* run, even on three legs."

"I need to tell you about Rachel," said Manny. "She's a rabbit who's bringing some weeds to help your wound heal. You think you should chase rabbits, of course, but she will help you, and you will be glad you did not chase her away."

"Chase a rabbit? I can't even raise my head. If she were *rabid*, I couldn't even *escape* from her, much less chase her." Dal not only sounded sad, but totally disheartened and beaten. And he continued to whimper.

Rachel arrived with some foam flower and addressed Dal in the authoritarian tone of a head nurse. "I guess Manny's told you why I'm here. I have to say it's against my better judgment, but Manny said you saved him from a snake. Obviously, in your current condition, you are not particularly frightening—not that dogs ever frighten me. I just run to get exercise and to keep the dogs from getting too fat for their own good."

Dal looked miserable. The pain told every muscle not to move, not to stir, not to resist its sovereignty. The pain was everywhere and nowhere, shrouding the space within and all around him. "I don't know what you're doing here," he said at last, "and if I bore any resemblance to myself, I'd chase you away as fast as you could run. Maybe I'd eat you, too, though I'd rather have canned chicken livers. That's my favorite."

"Dal," interrupted Manny. "Remember what I told you about the weeds? Maia and I are going to chew them into a paste and put it in your wound. It may hurt a little. You need to be brave like you were yesterday."

"I can't believe it. Me, a proud Dalmatian known for speed and aggression, a hunting hound specimen envied by all the other species of dog, reduced to an immobile heap, reduced to lectures on how to care for myself from mice and rabbits. It's too indignant. I think I shall die from the embarrassment to my spirit, rather than from the injury to my body."

Rachel thought of letting him have it about being a mongrel and not a Dalmatian, but she held her tongue. "You did a nice job of keeping the wound clean, Dal," she said, instead.

Dal reminded Rachel of all the things she disliked about domesticated dogs—self-centered, self-pitying animals, idly threatening to eat all kinds of things they had lost the hunger for. *Animals should eat to survive*, she thought. *It's unnatural to be served food from a can or a bag, and the result is clearly detrimental to the animal's character and intelligence. She felt a little resentful at this whole endeavor to help save this mutt. What had Dal done for her?* But she remembered that she was really helping Manny, who had saved her life.

Maia took on the task of placing the paste in the wound. Dal was a terrible patient. He complained non-stop about the pain, about the indignity of being nursed by mice and a rabbit, and about his bleak future as a three-legged dog.

"What if Farmer Frank takes me back to the pound? I didn't like it there. It smelled bad. There was no room to run and play. Most of the dogs seemed depressed. The ones who weren't, yapped non-stop, and the place was full of cats, as well. They were right there, but I couldn't get to them, couldn't chase them, couldn't steal their food or anything fun like that. Why would Farmer Frank keep a three-legged dog? Every fat rabbit in the neighborhood will be waltzing into the garden for a free lunch right under my nose. I may have to take *myself* to the pound to save any shred of self-respect."

Rachel felt provoked and bit down hard on her tongue, though Dal looked and sounded so pathetic it was hard for her to work up much animosity toward him. And she had to admit that she liked her role of healer. It didn't matter that the recipient of her wisdom and diligence was ungrateful.

Maia was as gentle as she could be. She whispered soothing words to let Dal know the paste was about to touch him, that he should be brave, that the application would make him strong again, would make him the fastest three-legged dog on the planet. Her words probably helped, but you wouldn't have known it by listening to Dal. He whined and moaned, mostly.

"And who would ever take a three-legged dog home with them from the pound?" he wailed at one point. "And what happens if no one takes you?"

The windless air suspended the question as though tracing each of its letters with the care deserving of the question's gravity, and even Rachel felt sympathy for this self-pitying dog with the leg that might heal but would never bear weight again.

When Dal complained of hunger and thirst, Manny told him they would be home before he could die of either, but he didn't feel as confident as he wanted to sound. What was needed, he felt, was something to boost Dal's spirits, something to make him want to get up and move on. The wound was bad, but the spirit needed healing even more.

"Dal," he said at last, "we're going to get you back to Farmer Frank's, back to protecting the garden against the incursions of vegetarians. Without you, Farmer and Mrs. Frank might have nothing to eat. Consider how hungry you are right now. Doesn't feel very good, does it? Well, poor Farmer and Mrs. Frank could feel that way all the time without you to protect the garden. They're depending on you."

Incursions of vegetarians? Something about the phrase seemed inappropriately pejorative to Rachel. "I'd just like to clear the air a little here," she said, unable to hold her annoyance. "I don't see the problem with a few of us who are designed to live on vegetables, rather than on dog food that may contain who knows what, helping ourselves to the excess produce grown by Farmer Frank. I think even Dal has probably observed—though I don't know how observant dogs really are—that a good deal of Farmer Frank's produce rots in the garden before he picks it. If we did not eat what we need, the only thing gained, so far as I can see, would be that even more of it would rot."

"But guarding the garden is the reason Farmer Frank brought me from the pound. I have to do that. If I ever get back there, that is." He whimpered again.

"Look," said Maia, "Manny didn't mean there was anything wrong with your trips to the garden, Rachel. And no one wants to deprive you of your job, Dal. The truth is that rabbits were eating vegetables in Farmer Frank's garden even when you had four good legs. Did Farmer Frank fire you when you didn't come back with a rabbit in your mouth? No. And he's not going to do so now. But Rachel here is getting older, so you have to promise that no matter how fast you get on your three legs, you will never close in and bite her."

"I don't know if I can do that. I mean, when I get going on the trail of a rabbit, my mind is on catching it, period."

"This is pointless," said Rachel. "There is no way a three-legged dog is going to catch me anyway. I don't need some kind of agreement. I'm safe in my superiority, thank you."

"No," said Manny. "Maia is right. It's the principle of it. We all need each other. No animal walks alone without fear. I've been with you Rachel. You can say you're not afraid. So can I. But we know fear. Fear is our friend, even if it's not a companion of choice. We should pledge to help and never do harm one to another. I'm placing my paw on Dal's, and that is my pledge. Rachel, Maia, place your paws on top of mine."

Rachel hesitated. Maia put her paw on Manny's. Reluctantly, Rachel put hers on Maia's. Manny led them in saying, "We pledge to help and never do harm one to another." The warmth of their touching bonded them as much as the words.

Manny and Maia crowded into the crevice where Dal had curled his neck toward his front legs to allow his head to rest close to his body. Rachel hesitated, but joined them, and Dal gave her an affectionate lick of his tongue that almost sent her away in disgust. But she stayed.

She felt every year of her advancing age, and she was thinking to next spring when Farmer Frank's organically grown new lettuce would surprise her mouth with a smoky aftertaste hinting of mulch. She thought it would be wonderful to know that Dal would give her some extra time to let her tongue roll over the flavors as her nose savored the scent. Nothing could compete in aroma with a sprouting garden in a spring breeze.

Dal lay listening to the throbbing wound echo in his head. His thoughts too turned to the garden, to his house with the warm blanket, to his feeding and water dishes. He would return. He had important work to do. He would guard the vegetables and chase Rachel and her family with a low growl and a powerful bark. And he would not catch them.

Everyone had fallen asleep, except Rachel, when the noise first filtered among the treetops. "Wake up," she said. "I hear a dog coming."

"That's a dog all right," said Dal. "It's Rusty; I can smell him. And Farmer Frank too."

They were coming fast, and even Manny and Maia, whose ears and noses were not as good as those of their canine and rabbit friends, could now hear the bark of the dog and see the shadow of a man coming across the cornfield with a dog well out in front.

"They're looking for you, Dal," said Manny. "We need to hide."

"So long Dal," said Rachel. "Hope your leg gets better." And she meant it.

"I won't forget our agreement. Come and have some vegetables whenever you want. And when I get fast again, I'll pretend I can't catch you."

You wish, thought Rachel, but she didn't say it. "Don't worry; you'll see plenty of me in the garden. I plan to be around awhile—and hungry too."

Dal raised himself up on his front legs and barked. Rusty barked in response and when he arrived, they licked and smelled each other enthusiastically. "Why didn't you come home, Dal?" asked Farmer Frank as he approached. He didn't see the wound until he reached down to pet Dal's head. "Wow, that's a really deep wound. You tangled with something nasty. We need to get you to the vet." He picked Dal up in his arms and Rusty followed them.

From their hiding place, Manny, Maia, and Rachel watched until Farmer Frank had crossed the corn field. "Let's go," said Manny.

On the return, Rachel carried Manny and Maia on her back and hopped slowly. The cold was not kind to her hip. Still, in a short time, they emerged from the cornfield and onto the raised ground of the fence-line just south of the leaning fencepost where they parted company and agreed to visit one another soon.

23. Partnership

At the woodpile, Manny led Maia onto his porch. They squeezed together against the cold and looked south toward the trees. No raccoon's eyes watched them. No stars offered light. No wind carried off their wisps of breath.

"What are you thinking?" asked Maia.

"I was thinking that we were lucky to make it here alive."

"Doesn't it seem like a long time since we met? I can hardly remember my life before this journey. I have a song for us."

> *Rest your head, upon my heart,*
> *To say that, we'll never part.*
> *Let me hear, the timing beat,*
> *Of our pul - ses where they meet.*
> *Rest your head, on me each night,*
> *So I'll know, that we're all right.*
> *With our bod - ies toasty warm,*
> *We can wea - ther every storm.*

Manny looked at Maia and she at him. He pretended to watch something out in the blackness beyond them. Only he could see nothing except Maia. She was next to him and all around him. He could not see into the night.

"Will you marry me?" he asked at last.

"Of course, I will. Why did you wait so long to ask?"

"I was afraid."

"Afraid I would say no?"

"I watched my brother die. I could have died several times. If you marry me, I want to enjoy it for a long time."

"I want to enjoy us for however long we have, even if our time is short."

They pressed together, pretending to watch the stars or the moon or the silhouettes of the trees to the south. And neither felt a trace of the cool night air.

"Let's go," Manny said after awhile. "I want my family to meet you."

They ran deep in among the rotted wood. Manny could smell fresh grass, the signal that the spirit of a disappeared loved one was being called home. If the grass had been placed in the nest to call *his* spirit home, it would be a great surprise when he entered the nest.

Everyone was sleeping. Manny saw his mother, his father, Bouqueet, and Shyleen. But Caressa was missing.

Manny nudged his mother gently. "Mother, it's me. I have a surprise for you. Her name is Maia."

"What...what...oh, Manny, it's you." She cried as she held him. "I was sure you had disappeared."

Everyone woke up and crowded around as Manny related all that had happened since he had been carried away by the hawk, slipping in, somewhere in the telling, that he and Maia would be getting married, and they would be inviting his friends, Gophericious, Rachel, and Dal. Everyone noticed Maia's tufts of white hair on her feet that looked especially feminine and her eyes that sparkled like their mothers.

Martha sobbed through most of the telling. She cried because Manny had returned, because Maia seemed like the only mouse she would have chosen for him, and because Caressa was not there. "All the friends you've made. It's wonderful how they've helped you and you've helped them," she said, at last.

"Where's Caressa?" asked Manny softly, hesitantly.

Martha looked at the ground. So did Fred. Bouqueet looked at Shyleen, and Shyleen began the story. "She asked me to go back with her. Everything seemed normal. We found Maggie in the kitchen and Alvin eating chocolate. We had a good visit and ate a lot. Winnie was there too and Triple M, or Mud, or whatever his real name is. I think he has a crush on Bouqueet."

Bouqueet turned away, and Shyleen continued. "Maggie told us we'd come on the right night, because Mrs. Frank had been sorting clothes and some were in a pile on the floor. There was a small, beautiful piece of silk right on top, and we had it out of the bedroom in a minute—not at all difficult or dangerous.

"It had all been so easy in the house. I guess that's why we got careless outside. We had barely started pulling the silk across the field when the owl had her. Caressa cried out. I couldn't move. The owl flew off with her but landed just a short distance away. When I saw the owl snap its head down to eat, I turned away and hid until morning."

"The silk of Caressa's obsession," said Manny, looking at the rumpled ball of silk in the corner of the nest. "I never noticed texture until she pointed it out to me."

"I have cried enough," said Martha. "Death is a presence we have to accept. But Caressa's spirit is alive and with us. Last night at dusk I sat on your porch with a small piece of the silk, and as I sat watching the dark call the stars to the sky, I could feel her presence."

Martha paused, wiped her tears, and continued, "It's time to turn to the joy in our lives. The joy of Manny and Maia. We must plan the wedding. What's this about Gopherisus—or however you pronounce his name—and Rachel coming to the wedding? And Dal? What are you thinking?"

"I know it sounds impossible and weird. But these animals have been so important to Manny's life—and to mine too. They have to be at the wedding," said Maia.

"Well, that's totally preposterous," said Fred, tugging on the white hairs on his chin. "A dog at a mouse wedding? Don't be ridiculous. No one would come, and I wouldn't either."

"You can stay home, if you wish," said Martha, "but it sounds like you'll miss out on something special."

24. Enlisting Help

Manny and Maia slept through the day. When they awoke, they went back to the porch and watched the flurry of dusk play out around them. A flock of geese flew overhead toward the lake in the pasture where Maia's parents lived. Deer appeared in the cornfield. A hundred Blackbirds found a home in the oak trees. Rabbits scampered for warrens. Groundhogs scurried for cover. Creatures who hoped to sleep on a full stomach ate their last bites anxiously—prepared to flee at any movement of dried leaf in sundown air, any crack of twig, any whiff of danger's smell at this moment when the day and night predators converged for dinner.

These sounds, sights, and smells of life were in full when the noise broke across the sky. In the dusk air, it rolled in low as though channeled by a glass ceiling suspended just above the tree-tops and way below the canvas where the clouds could be painted or the stars hung out to shine. The noise began distant and picked up roar as it came, slowly filling the horizon with a tractor, black smoke, Farmer Frank hunkered under a parka hood, a flat-bed trailer piled high with rocks, and a dog running along beside.

Manny and Maia watched as this noisy, trackless train passed north of the woodpile toward the farmhouse where the rock rabbit ears of which Rachel had spoken rose well into the sky. Maia knew what it meant. "Farmer Frank must have taken away every rock from the wall. My family must be homeless. I need to go back and bring them here for our wedding and to live here too."

"It's too dangerous. I won't let you go alone."

"You should stay here. Your mother needs you."

"No, she doesn't. She's strong. To get there and back again, we'll need each other and maybe more."

"Dal could carry us back. A three-legged dog can still run faster than we can."

"He's not really a three-legged dog yet. He's a badly wounded dog. He may not be walking at all."

"What about Rusty?" asked Maia. "We made friends with Dal. Why not with Rusty? He goes to the pasture with Farmer Frank. He knows exactly where to go."

"I don't think we can just walk up to Rusty and ask him to carry us out to the rock wall and back. The way we made friends with Dal was that *he* needed *us*. I don't think it would have worked the other way around."

"It can't hurt to try, can it?"

"Well, it can if Rusty decides to bite first and listen later."

"What if we asked Dal to ask him? Dal and Rusty must be friends."

"Great idea. I'll talk to Dal about it." He bumped Maia lovingly and was gone.

In the cold night, Manny took the shortest route to the house, not following the fence but running across the open pasture directly to the lower part of the garden, to the barrier that didn't want to be crossed. The song in his head replaced the ache in his lungs before he found himself breathing fast and looking up at the scarecrow, smiling at him, welcoming him, showing she was happy to see him. And the fence no longer said, "Do not cross me." It was just wire and posts without a mission.

Next to the house, Manny could see the two giant rock ears rising from the ground and joined to each other at the base by a rock enclosure. Manny thought not a rock could be left in the far pasture. The smashed kitchen door of the house opening onto the back porch had been replaced with a new one that had both a dog and a cat door in it. Dal's house had been moved onto the porch.

Manny looked up at the scarecrow one last time and ran into the garden past the lettuce and carrots, past the melons and cornstalks, past the cabbages, and on up to the far end of the garden where the scarecrow with the furrowed brow stood guard but also appeared to welcome him. Manny could see the outline of Dal inside the dog house on the porch. "Dal, Dal, it's me, Manny," he yelled as he scrambled up the steps.

A faint, yet positive, grunt came from inside the dog house. "How's the leg?" Manny asked.

"It's bad. I can't use it at all. Farmer Frank's been very good to me, though. I don't think he's going to take me back to the pound. I've been getting all my favorite foods from cans. Look at the bandage on my leg. The vet did that. It hurt at the time, but the pain is pretty much gone."

"Can you walk at all?"

"Once I get up, I can hobble a little. Farmer Frank lifts me off the porch in the morning and again in the evening so I can go to the bathroom. Look at the blankets in my dog house. They're all wool."

"I have a favor to ask. You know how you and Rusty followed Farmer Frank to the rock wall in the far pasture? Maia's family lives among those rocks—or, at least, they did. They may be homeless now. Maia wants to go back and bring them here."

"That's a long ways for a mouse to travel. No offense, but you mice don't have very long legs—though I know yours are really strong."

"And I forgot the most important part. Maia and I are getting married, and we want you to come to the wedding."

"That's great. I'd love to come. Where will it be?"

"Weddings are held in the hollow log corridor inside the woodpile, but you wouldn't be able to get in there. I just thought of that."

"Why don't you have it here on the porch? We'll spread out my wool blankets so the guests have warm feet. And I'll howl at the moon to scare away evil spirits. That's what we do at dog weddings. Everyone howls at the moon. It's a lot of fun, really. I don't think my bad leg will affect my howling. I'm pretty good at it."

"Great idea, Dal, but first, Maia wants to bring her family here."

"What do you want me to do?"

"Well, you know how we rode on your back?"

"But I can't even get down off this porch."

"I wasn't thinking of you. I know you would if you could. I was thinking of Rusty. I was hoping you would ask him for us."

"Sure, I'd be glad to. He can bark pretty mean, but it's all bark. I've never seen him catch or do harm to anything— only don't tell him I said that. We can talk to him in the morning. Come sleep in my house. I've got three wool blankets."

Dal's body heat filled the dog house, the warmth covering Manny with a blanket of sleep. He dreamed of the magic world of Zeus.

* * *

Zeus was not sure he was comfortable with the changes taking place in his world. After successfully protecting mice lo these many years—indeed since time immemorial as far as he could determine—Athena was introducing changes that were not entirely to his liking, although he had to acknowledge some evidence of their effectiveness—at least in the short term.

The unsettling change was Athena's objection to corporal punishment. Athena had introduced "time-out" as a punishment for predators caught considering a lunch of mouse—or a breakfast or dinner for that matter. Athena was using her magic powers to confine offenders to corners where they were required to stay for varying periods of time, depending on the seriousness of their offense. If a predator had only thought of a mouse mousse dessert, but not yet acted upon the thought in any threatening manner, the duration of time-out might be fairly short. The predator would be given the benefit of the doubt.

"After all," Athena said, "You can't prove a negative, now can you?"

She said it with such authoritative conviction that Zeus was left without a response. He was sure there must be a way to prove a negative, to show that proving a negative wasn't actually the issue, or possibly that proving a negative was not appropriate to the situation, but he was unable to make an effective argument for any of these positions.

"You haven't actually changed the nature of cats by punching them in the nose, now have you?" Athena asked. "And these threats of turning carnivorous beasts into vegetarians surely are not serious? Not that you couldn't do it. But sometimes, we have to refrain from imposing our will on others in order for them to accept that doing what we want is also what they want. You do understand what I'm talking about, don't you?"

"Of course, I do," said Zeus, but he didn't. "Nevertheless, I don't see the harm in turning a fox into a vegetarian. What could possibly be wrong with that?"

"Well, for one thing, it's unnatural. It's not clear to me what would happen to the earth if we succeeded in eliminating all the carnivores. Mother Earth might not like it, and it could have unforeseen negative consequences for mice."

"Well, there are some modifications to Mother Earth that seem potentially to be of great benefit to mice."

Athena rolled her eyes. She loved Zeus. He had a heart of gold, fundamentally. But he was impatient. She believed in gradual changes—some of which could be negotiated and some of which would occur naturally, if you were patient. Zeus was inclined to resolve conflicts and administer justice with force. Athena believed such methods belonged to the past. "If you throw your magic powers around indiscriminately, you will never achieve your goal of harmony among the creatures of the earth. No one will listen. Of course, they will pretend to, because you have the magic rod. But will they really change?"

"Well, if I weren't throwing my magic powers around—as you have chosen to characterize the deft and judicious manner in which I administer justice and exercise dominion—how many mice do you think would be left on this earth?"

"Probably a rather large number, but that is not the point. The point is the quality of life of those present."

"All I know is that I have saved the life of many a mouse, and I plan to continue to do that. It feels good. The mice are grateful, and the bad guys suffer. It's the natural order of how to be a super hero."

"It's not the saving of mice that I object to. I'm all in favor of that. The issue is whether you can save mice by changing the basic nature of other animals through the use of corporal punishment—bashing of heads to be precise."

"I haven't just spent my time bashing heads as you call it. I have a whole arsenal of punishments. Sometimes I hold their mouth shut so they can't breathe until they promise to change their ways. Sometimes I simply confuse their taste buds so that the thought of eating mice makes them gag. Sometimes I whirl them around until they get sick. Sometimes, it's true, I might smack them in the nose a little or crack them in the air. It gets their attention, and it's not like it kills them or anything."

"Surely you don't believe that a fox's promise to change its ways can be accepted at face value. What happens when you turn your back?"

"Well, I can't do everything. There are too many of them."

"My point exactly. Since we can only have a limited impact for a limited period of time, a non-physical approach, such as time-out, works just as effectively as a bop on the head. Animals hate to be confined. They don't like to be in time-out. It gives them just as much pause to reconsider their ways as does corporal punishment."

Zeus was getting a headache. He hated policy discussions.

* * *

"Wake up, Manny," said Dal. "Rusty's coming. Rusty! Rusty, come over here. I need to talk to you."

"Just a minute. Let me go to the bathroom first." Rusty was still pretty agile going up and down steps once he got moving, but first thing in the morning was hard. His legs got stiff overnight and the joints didn't want to bend where they were supposed to. He whimpered a little as he went down the steps.

The door to the house opened and Farmer Frank came out. He was wearing a dark terry-cloth robe, wool-lined slippers, and a stocking cap. His frame was bent, and he looked harmless.

"Farmer Frank's coming," said Dal. "You'd better hide."

Manny crawled to the back and under the edge of the top blanket, and Dal pulled himself up as Farmer Frank reached in to help him to his feet. Farmer Frank was so close Manny could smell the pipe on his breath. He had a hard time not laughing.

"Come on, boy," said Farmer Frank, "Let's get you up and going here."

Farmer Frank carried Dal down the steps, and Dal hobbled over next to Rusty by the garden fence. Within a few minutes, Dal and Rusty came back together. Manny thought Rusty looked puzzled and unconvinced. Farmer Frank lifted Dal onto the porch and went back inside the house.

"Okay, let's go over this again," said Rusty. "You want me to carry two mice back to where we go with Farmer

Frank to get the rocks, and then you want me to carry maybe a dozen mice back from there. Why should I do that?"

"Because those mice saved my life," said Dal. "One of them is right here in my dog house with me. Come on out, Manny. Rusty won't hurt you."

Manny crawled out from under the blanket. "Hello, Rusty. Glad to meet you. I really would be very grateful if you would help us bring Maia's family here. Maia and I are getting married, and she wants her family to be here."

"It's not hard to carry mice," said Dal. "Heck, I did it with only three legs. You'll be going back out there again anyway. It won't hurt for a couple of mice to ride on your back."

"Well, that's easy for you to say. You were wounded and probably delirious. Dogs are not beasts of burden. What if someone saw me? How would I explain what I was doing?"

"Who's going to see you? You're always dreaming that some frilly French poodle is going to show up and ask for a home here. But the odds of that happening are not good— least of all on the one time you're carrying mice!"

"If we see another dog coming," said Manny, "Maia and I will get down and hide until they go away. Mice can disappear right in front of your eyes."

"But you can't escape a dog's nose," said Rusty. "Any dog would smell you. I'd be the first dog they ever met who smelled like a mouse. How embarrassing would that be?"

"Look Rusty," said Dal. "It's a favor to me. That's all it is. We dogs have to stick together. I took over the garden-watching duties for you, didn't I?"

"All right, I'll do it. But you owe me one."

"Thank you," said Manny. "Maybe some day I can help you too."

"A mouse help a dog? Not likely. I won't waste time waiting for help from you, though I understand you somehow did help Dal, here."

"You know the big woodpile down the fence-line?"

"Of course. I know every inch of this farm."

"Maia and I will be waiting on the cold wind side of the woodpile."

"I'll be there, but for now, you'd better hide. Farmer Frank doesn't like mice."

Manny disappeared below the edge of the porch just as Farmer Frank came out. "Here you go, Dal," he said. "Canned chicken livers mixed in with 100% protein-based dried dog food for healthy and happy dogs. That's what it says on the bag, you lucky dog."

Manny ran for the woodpile, unseen and without fear, a mouse high on the joy of fresh air and earth's aromas, a mouse flying just above the realm of field and house to the land where Zeus protected the mice of the world.

* * *

Zeus was setting new standards for industriousness. He spent less time lecturing animals and attempting to appeal to their limited powers of reasoning and, instead, simply administered punishments swiftly and fairly. Time-out had not completely displaced other forms of punishment, but it played a large part in his scheme of enforcement. The thing he liked about it was its efficiency. He didn't have to waste time and energy carrying animals up in the air and twirling them round and round until they became green, barfed, and begged for mercy. One sharp point of the magic rod and a quick command was all it took. Zap, "You there, 20 minutes in time-out." Bingo, it was done, and Zeus was off to the next crime scene.

Athena had some reservation that he was administering justice a little too swiftly, a little too joyfully, and not always with an adequate standard of evidence, but she accepted that, on balance, the system was working, and their regime was gaining broad respect as fair and just. She loved Zeus, and their partnership made possible what neither of them could achieve alone.

* * *

When Manny arrived at the woodpile, Maia was waiting on the porch. "Did Rusty agree to carry us?"

"Yes, but he's not thrilled about it."

They did not have to wait long before the noise of Farmer Frank's tractor heading for the far pasture confirmed that there were still remnants of the rock wall there, and Maia's family might be in it. Rusty was following the trailer but turned toward where they were waiting and arrived with his tongue dripping slobber. Manny looked at Rusty as though seeing him for the first time. He looked remarkably unfrightening, though he smelled bad. His hair was a disheveled mess with burrs and other bits of weeds stuck in it. The hair was too long for his size. He looked like a mix between a large breed with long hair and a small breed with short hair that had split the difference on size but kept a length of hair that belonged to a bigger frame. It was not a result Manny thought flattered Rusty.

"Thanks for coming," he said. "Rusty, this is Maia. Maia, this is Rusty. Is it all right for us to get on your back now?"

"Yes, of course, I'm a dog of my bark. I'm beginning to think I'm not so smart a dog as I thought I was to be talked into this, but I agreed, and that's that. Sorry, Maia, please excuse my bad manners. Pleased to meet you. Dal told me that you and Manny may have saved his life. When you're a young dog, chasing everything that moves, you can get yourself killed before experience puts some sense in your head. He was lucky. Hop aboard. You can run right up my tail onto my back. My beautiful long hair will be easy for you to grip onto."

25. Reunion

The tractor's growl now seemed familiar to Maia and less frightening. Nevertheless, she had no love for it. She tried not to be angry with Farmer Frank, but the whole project was so puzzling, so irrational, so pointless. What could be the purpose of piling the rocks up toward the sky in the farmyard?

"Rusty," she yelled, "how much of the rock wall is left in the pasture?"

"Not a lot. About the length of four dogs, head to tail."

They rode in silence, the landmarks passing quickly: the cornfield, the small cluster of trees by the fence, and the hay field. The tractor's engine formed a cocoon of sound that focused the thoughts of all present each into himself.

Maia felt some relief in Rusty's report of a partial wall remaining in the far pasture. It could mean that her family was still in it. But if they had been dispersed, some of them might not have found safe hiding places.

Rusty was obsessing about being a beast of burden and what it would look like if he were seen by the frilly French poodle of his dreams. He was also worrying about his status generally. He was used to being the senior dog. He was no longer expected to do much of anything, except look up appreciatively every time Farmer or Mrs. Frank looked at him, spoke to him, put out his food, or asked him to take them for a walk. But now that Dal had only three legs, would they expect *him* to go back to guarding the garden? The excitement of chasing everything that moved or seemed frightened of him had lost its appeal. Would they bring in another dog? Was there enough food for another dog?

Farmer Frank was thinking about the new house. He'd promised Mrs. Frank that they would move into the new house and rent out the old one, but somehow the new house was ending up bigger than the one in which they'd raised their children. It didn't make sense, but it was too late to do the sensible thing. The house was prefabricated and would be arriving the next morning.

The one part he really liked was the rock-work. He was proud of how he had used the rock from these walls, which were no longer of use as fences, to make chimneys, facing for the foundation, and a historically accurate reproduction rock fence between the two houses.

Manny was thinking about what would happen when they got to the wall. He had not counted on Farmer Frank. He couldn't see how they'd be able to get off Rusty's back and find Maia's family without Farmer Frank seeing them.

They entered the far pasture. There were geese on the water and more on the land searching for food in the grass. The sentries moved uneasily at the sound and sight of the tractor. They watched the tractor and moved impatiently, steadily building to a decision. At last, one sentry arched its wings and began a laborious lift, followed by another, and another, and another, until the whole flock was lifting, pumping, pushing, struggling to get airborne. Their take-off was not graceful in the way Manny remembered them flying in formation high against the sky. In take-off, their effort was of bodies too heavy for the span of their wings.

"I don't think my family will be in the rock wall. They will have left as soon as they heard the tractor," said Maia.

"With my nose, I'll be able to track them easily," said Rusty. "I chase scents all the time out here; Farmer Frank won't suspect anything."

The tractor came to a stop a short distance from the wall, and Rusty picked up the scent of mice.

The scent was leading toward the multiflora rose bushes where Manny and Maia had met. "Stop, Rusty," said Maia. "My family will be afraid of you. They'll scatter if you get any closer. Manny and I will go on from here."

"Mom, Dad," yelled Maia, as they neared the rosebushes. "We came back to take you to a safe place."

"It's Maia," yelled Linda, Maia's mother. She came running out from among the thorns of the rosebushes to hug Maia and Manny. "I never thought I'd see you again. It's been a terrible time. The farmer kept coming back. He took every rock from the wall where we had lived for generations, and he's almost finished taking all the rocks from the older wall too. Take us to a safe place? What do you mean?"

"Farmer Frank's dog is with us," said Maia. "His name is Rusty. He's agreed to carry us to where Manny's family lives."

Tanya, Gary, and Robert, Maia's father, came out to meet them and everyone hugged. "Where are Jim and Gloria?" asked Maia.

There was a moment of silence. "We've had a hard time since you left," her mother, Linda, said, at last. "Your father and I..."

It was Tanya who continued, "We had to leave the rock fence to find new nest material every time Farmer Frank removed more of the wall. It was dangerous work. We're the only ones left."

Maia hugged her mother and father, her brother and sister; they cried quietly. Manny felt uncomfortable but also unsure what he should say or do. Everyone became quiet, as though waiting for a sign until the powerful smell of dogbreath announced Rusty's approach.

"Rusty's coming," said Maia. "He looks frightening, but he won't harm us."

"Pleased to meet you," said Rusty, as he arrived. "I hope you understand. I mean, I don't want to complain. I did agree to this, but this is not something I intend to make a habit. It's useful for a dog to wander far and wide following scents that otherwise would simply be without purpose. But it's not natural for a dog to carry mice on his back while he's doing it."

"Oh yes," said Maia, "we're most grateful for your help and would never abuse your kindness. Anyway, it's not natural for mice to wander around aimlessly following scents—not that we don't appreciate the value in your doing that—but since it's not something *we* do, we would never ask to come with you."

"This is it," said Manny. "One trip. Just like we agreed."

"Okay, okay. I'm sorry to make a fuss about it. It's just that if someone saw me..." The words were left unspoken but his thought was of the frilly French poodle of his dreams waltzing into his life, saying, "Hi, big guy, got a place a lady could hang her hat?"

The words that actually carried across and through the rosebushes were ordinary but could not have sounded more sublime to Rusty. "Excuse me, I heard you talking to the mice," came a soft dog's voice. "You seem like a kind dog, and my friend and I have been seeking kindness unsuccessfully for what seems a very long time. Do you know where we could find something to eat and a warm place to sleep?"

Rusty looked up, staring through the rosebushes. It sounded like a dog. It smelled like a dog. And though the rosebushes obstructed the view, it appeared to be a frilly French poodle! Rusty's knees suddenly lost the sinews that held him upright. He slowly sank to the ground, unable to speak, trying to make it look as though he was deliberately kneeling down to get a better view through the bushes. From ground level, he could see quite clearly that the dog on the other side was, indeed, a French poodle. He felt as though he might never be able to get up.

Fortunately, Manny broke the silence, "Yes, Rusty here is a very kind dog. I'm sure he will help you. Where he lives there's lots of food and a warm house too."

"Allow me," said Rusty, now jumping energetically to his feet. "I will, of course, be of every help that there is to be of where help is concerned," he said, a little too eagerly to get the sentence to come out right.

The French poodle that emerged from the other side of the rose bushes was not exactly a glamour queen among canines. Her hair was past needing a trim. The parts of her body that would have been properly trimmed had grown out an inch or more, and the parts that would have been left a couple of inches long were now unevenly shaggy, and clumped with burrs and weed bits. Rusty thought she looked gorgeous. She had lively eyes in which he saw himself reflected as the handsome young dog of her dreams. And she had the best set of legs he had ever seen.

"My name is Eva," she said, lowering her head ever so slightly to show her proper upbringing and membership among the trained of the canine world. "I must apologize for my appearance. I hardly know where to start. The beginning is really Fifi. Fifi, come join us."

Out from behind Eva, stepped a young dog with hair even more knotted up with burs and thistles than was Eva's. She had a poodle face but a smaller body size with ears, hair and tail that suggested an indeterminate mix of other dogs. "I'm Fifi," she said shyly. "I'm very pleased to meet you. I'm afraid everything is my fault. I didn't mean to be any trouble. I don't think I would have peed on the floor, except everyone was so excited. The people kept yelling and smacking the newspaper on the floor and sometimes on me. They even pushed my nose in the pee sometimes, as though I didn't know what pee was! I just feel so bad, especially for Eva. She didn't do anything wrong."

"It wasn't her fault, really," said Eva. "She tried; the people just didn't know how to help her. And the small child pulled our hair."

"How did you end up here in the fields?" asked Maia. "Rusty, here, has been very kind to us. I'm sure he will help you too. He's a remarkable dog with exceptional intelligence and a huge heart."

The praise caught Rusty off guard, but he recovered. "Oh my, I must say I have certainly forgotten my manners. My being here with these...these mice requires a bit of explanation. It isn't like I routinely associate with mice, I mean, like spend time with them or have them as friends or anything that might suggest... I mean, really, I'm a very regular kind of dog, basically. That is, regular with exceptional qualities, of course, for example..."

"Rusty *is* an exceptional dog," interrupted Manny. "He's been helping us, which not just any dog would do. If you need help, Rusty's the dog for it."

"Yes, of course," said Rusty, "Anything you need, I'm at your service. Did you say you have no home?"

"I don't quite know how to explain it. Our owners took us for a drive, a longer one than usual. Suddenly, they stopped and put Fifi outside. I didn't like the smell of the situation, so I jumped out too. They called for me to come back, but not for Fifi. It seemed to me they didn't wait very long. I considered following the scent of the car to get back home, but I thought I could help Fifi more if we were on our own. I didn't realize how hard it would be to find good food and a warm place to sleep."

"That's terrible," said Rusty, "What were they thinking? A dog has to have food brought to it twice a day." His stomach rumbled at even the thought of hunger.

"Maybe they were just putting Fifi out to be sure she wouldn't pee in the car. I don't know. It's been hard out here, but I like the freedom in the country. I'm hoping we can be taken in by a farmer. Farmers have lots of space, and Fifi can pee anywhere any time. But so far, everyone has chased us away."

"You're certainly welcome to live at our farm. There are two of us there. The other dog is young and part Dalmatian. His name's Dal. He thinks he's purebred Dalmatian, but he's not. He's had a nasty run-in with a bear that's left him with only three good legs. Still, in spite of his pretension to pedigree and having only three legs, he's a fine dog."

"Would the farmer want two more dogs?" asked Fifi.

"Well, Dal's misfortune might be one reason. Farmer Frank might welcome two more dogs to help with the guard duties. Personally, I've pretty much retired and limit myself mostly to supervising Dal. Of course, I don't mean that if you lived with us that I'd insist on over-lording things. Dal needs it, but I can see that you certainly do not. Anyway, I don't know why Farmer and Mrs. Frank would not be delighted to have two more dogs. We're very good to people. We love them more than they love each other, so what human would not welcome total adoration from more dogs?"

"I could just leave Fifi with you," suggested Eva. "Most people have a soft spot for young dogs but are suspicious of older dogs. I'll find a home somewhere."

"Don't be ridiculous; I won't hear of it. If Farmer and Mrs. Frank won't take both of you in, I'll find a farm that will take all of us."

Farmer Frank's voice rang out above the drone of the tractor's engine. "Come on Rusty. Leave those dogs alone."

The barely warming air of noon suspended the phrase "those dogs" across the green grass. No one moved. No eye strayed from Farmer Frank.

"Quick, Rusty," whispered Manny. "You go with Farmer Frank, so he doesn't get suspicious. We'll bring Eva and Fifi to the house after dark."

"Okay, if you promise to come to the farm," Rusty said looking directly at Eva.

"Count on it. We'll be there," she said.

Rusty ran toward the tractor as fast as he could go, as fast as if he were a two-year-old dog just reached his prime. It was hard for him to follow the tractor back to the farmyard. Every few steps, he cast a glance back toward the far pasture with the lake to see if Eva was coming. It wasn't that he didn't trust her to keep her word; it was just that he couldn't wait for it to happen.

In the excitement, his nose also found youth and pulled him to fragrances in every direction. A thousand more aromas than he'd remembered ever noticing before now urged him to follow them. It took every ounce of discipline he possessed to keep focused on the back of the flatbed and running true on the path that led to the farmyard. Considering how little discipline he possessed, Rusty's arrival back at the farm was a considerable accomplishment.

As they neared the farmyard, Rusty passed the tractor and went on ahead to the porch. "Dal, Dal," he yelled, panting heavily. "You won't believe it. Two French poodles are coming to live with us. Eva is the most beautiful dog ever. She'll live with me, of course. Her friend, Fifi, is young and probably not really a French poodle, but she has a certain charm. She's not trained, you know, about where to pee, so she'll have to live out here with you."

Rusty had rushed through the whole speech so rapidly Dal could hardly grasp the meaning. *Two French poodles coming to live with them? Surely, Rusty was joking. One would be an unbelievable stroke of luck, but two would have to be an apparition. Was Rusty losing touch with reality? Could he be sick?* Suddenly, his loss of a leg didn't seem so bad, compared to being delusional.

"What? What are you talking about?" he blurted out. "Where did you see these French poodles? If they exist, why can't I see them? Tell me you can't see them, because, believe me, they are not here."

"No, no, I know they're not here, as in right here at this moment. But they are in the far pasture with the lake, and they're coming; trust me. Oh, I'm so excited I can hardly believe it's true myself. Just wait until you lay your eyes on these beauties. Life is not going to be the same around here. Everything is about to change. I think I'll start by chasing Flora out of here. I never did like that cat."

"Don't get carried away, old man. Even if these poodles exist, they're not here, Farmer and Mrs. Frank have not agreed to let them stay, and you are no match for Flora. If you so much as growl at her sideways, your nose will end up a bloody mess, and you too embarrassed to show yourself to any frilly French poodle. Now slow down and tell me exactly what happened. Where are the mice?"

"Oh, yes, I forgot that part. It all kind of happened together, but Eva has made me forget everything else." Rusty went on to narrate the entire story, finishing with, "Eva and Fifi are bringing Manny, Maia, and her family here as soon as it's dark."

Dal could not imagine two French poodles coming across the nearest hill. How could that happen? Still, he wanted to believe it badly enough that he found his eyes following Rusty's gaze to the west, to the top of the horizon, to the birthplace from which fantasy was destined to arrive in the form of two French poodles.

26. The Refugees Arrive

Farmer Frank pulled the flatbed around to the partially-built rock wall that ran between the old house and the foundation of the new house. Then he hit the hydraulic lift to raise the front of the flatbed and dump the rocks on the ground. To the dogs, who would normally have found this of interest, it was, on this particular day, irrelevant noise and motion. Their eyes did not waver from the west's horizon. Farmer Frank put the tractor away and came walking back to the porch. He sat down next to the dogs and rubbed their heads.

"Nice to see you out of your house, Dal. You'll be ready to guard the garden soon. You never caught anything anyway, so you'll be about as useful with three legs as with four. All you have to do is bark. The rabbits won't know the difference. Maybe Rusty, here, could help out a little. With you being so energetic and running after everything, he's been getting old before his time. That can't be good for dogs. It's certainly not good for people."

He rubbed their heads once more and went into the house, returning after a few minutes with a dog treat for each of them and another rub on the head.

Back at the far pasture, Eva, Fifi, Manny, Maia and her family huddled together where the fence was overgrown with rosebushes, honeysuckle, and poison ivy and waited for dusk. Not much was spoken. Everyone in this huddled mass yearned to be accepted, to breathe without fear, to eat without hurry, to sleep without cold.

Robert, Maia's father, lay thinking about the uncertainty of finding a new home at the farm. *Would they have to become house mice? What did parents teach their children about living in a house?* It was not familiar to him.

Linda, Maia's mother, mourned quietly. She did not like leaving the area where some of her children had died. The rock wall had been full of spirits from many generations. She could not imagine living anywhere else.

As for Eva, she was feeling optimistic, despite her hunger and tiredness. Rusty inspired confidence. The worst thing that could happen, she felt, was that they might have to leave after a few days. But at least they might leave with full stomachs.

Maia was thrilled. She was sure that her parents, sister, and brother would find safe places to build nests at the farm.

Manny was focused on the immediate hours ahead of them. Maia's family would need nests. He would ask all the neighbors to help build them.

"Is it time to go?" Eva asked at last. "How long does it take to get to the farm?"

"Not long," said Manny. "We don't want to arrive before Farmer and Mrs. Frank are in the house for the night."

"I don't think I can wait until then," said Fifi. "I need something to eat now."

"The sun's nearing the top of the mountain," said Maia. "We can leave shortly."

All of them sat watching the sun settle behind the trees at the top of the mountain. Its sparse warmth was gone even before its last rays filtered through the trees that formed the western horizon. "It's time to go," said Manny.

The unusual troop set off. Eva and Fifi walked side by side with the six mice dug into the hair on their backs. The travelers were poor and ill-kempt; some of them were hungry; all of them looked ahead into the approaching dark with anxiety and hope. They were not walking from the far pasture to the farmyard; they were walking to a new beginning. Except for Manny, they were refugees from homes to which they could not return. Their bodies needed food; their spirits, dignity.

As they walked, the sun pulled darkness behind it quickly. By the time they reached the horizon of the hill that Rusty and Dal were watching, the ballet of stars was already in progress on the sky's black stage.

"That's them. They're coming. They're coming!" yelled Rusty, turning round and round on the porch as though chasing his tail. "They're coming! I told you. I told you. Can you believe it? Do you see them? Do you believe me now? Come on, let's go meet them," he said, forgetting that Dal could not get off the porch by himself.

Dal did not want the poodles to think him an invalid. He put one front leg down onto the first step, then the other, and repeated it for the second step, leaving his back legs on the porch. He made a small jump with his good rear leg. To his surprise, the leg landed safely on the first step. The rest was easy.

Meanwhile, Rusty had reached the top of the hill where the refugees waited. "You're right on time," he said. "You will love it on Farmer Frank's farm."

"Are you sure we'll be welcome?" asked Eva, skeptically. "Not everyone..."

"Nonsense," said Rusty, "who wouldn't want a wonderful dog like you? Or even young Fifi, here? There's a lot of work for dogs on a farm. I bark whenever someone comes in the driveway. I keep Farmer Frank company pretty much wherever he goes. I guard the bedroom all night. I eat the food that falls off the table. I protect the farm from bears, bobcats, groundhogs, squirrels, deer, and all manner of ill-intentioned creatures. Really, if the Franks consider for one minute all the dog work around the farm, they'll be happy to have two more of us."

Manny looked at the house. The lights in the windows spotted the darkness, revealing the outline of the house and the rock chimneys against the sky not far from it, but little else. Tonight, the house held much the same mystery for Manny that it had the night he had seen it for the first time. It did not look familiar or inviting.

"The Franks' house looks frightening; but if you're careful, it's safe enough," he said to no one in particular.

"My mother told stories she'd heard about living in a house," said Linda, Maia's mother. "I thought she did it to frighten us children from venturing too far from the rock wall. The stories certainly never made me want to be a house mouse."

"We'll be safe," said Maia. "Manny knows this farm well. See the rock ears sticking into the air not far from the house? Those were made with the rocks from our wall. I think it's a good omen. We're coming home, sort of."

To Eva, the house looked small and unsubstantial. She had come from a city, from life in a high-rise building. Against the black of a moon-less sky, this small shadow that cast its polka dots of light into oblivion seemed to Eva to offer more illusion than safety.

The troop approached from the direction that took them past President Abraham Lincoln, the scarecrow with the worried brow. In the darkness, its shadow loomed as a sentry, guarding the farm entrusted to it, blocking access to a new life.

"Is he upset with me?" asked Fifi when she saw the scarecrow. "I won't pee here. I can hold it. I don't want him to be angry. He looks angry."

"No," said Manny. "He's not upset with you. He just worries a lot. The garden is a big responsibility, I think. Look, here comes Dal."

Dal moved slowly. He took short steps with his front legs and brought his back half forward by hopping on his one good leg, the other hanging by his side.

Everyone was introduced. Dal thought Fifi was the perfect dog to share his dog house, but he did not say that. Instead, he launched into his misfortune and how he would be back to full running form in short order, although his voice lacked conviction on this latter point.

"If you need anything that requires running, I'm very good at that," said Fifi. "Actually, I get a little too eager sometimes. That was what got me into trouble where we lived. You see..."

"Never mind," interrupted Eva to save Fifi embarrassment, "there will be plenty of time to share our life stories."

"It's time to go to the house," said Dal. "Farmer Frank will come outside to smoke his pipe. He'll expect to find me there. I let him scratch my head while he smokes. And he puts out my food and water dishes. I don't want to miss that."

"Did you say food and water?" asked Fifi. "Can I please have some of your food? I won't eat a lot. I'm not a big dog, but I haven't eaten for a long time. My head hurts and I feel dizzy."

"Of course, you can have it all. I won't eat anything," said Dal, forgetting that he possessed no discipline and would never be able to refrain from eating. "You all go on ahead," he continued. "I don't want to hold anyone up."

"I'll stay with you," said Fifi.

"No," said Manny, "You and Eva need to run fast and hide under the porch before Farmer Frank comes out to smoke. I don't think it would be good to surprise Farmer Frank tonight."

"That's right," said Rusty. "I certainly don't want him to see us bringing him a bunch of mice. It's nothing personal, you understand. But I remember a night when some mice in the house caused a lot of trouble for Farmer and Mrs. Frank. Farmer Frank would reject Eva and Fifi for sure, if he caught them bringing mice to the house. Let's go."

Rusty led Fifi and Eva under the porch. Dal was still making his way back when Farmer Frank came out. "Dal? Is that you?" he said. "Good for you, boy. You got down off the porch all by yourself."

Farmer Frank went back into the house and returned with Dal's food and water dishes, put them down, sat on the edge of the porch, and lit his pipe. "Rusty, where have you been?" he said as Rusty came around the corner. "Your food is in the kitchen."

Rusty sat down beside Farmer Frank to give him a chance to scratch his head. Rusty thought Farmer Frank should be reminded especially tonight of all the pleasures dogs brought to his life. "You did hear me say your food was waiting, didn't you?" Farmer Frank asked.

Food was one of the first words Rusty had learned. Normally, it would have sent him dashing into the kitchen. But not tonight. Tonight he rubbed against Farmer Frank and tried to clean his face in spite of the fact that the pipe smelled horrible. *At least I don't smell mice droppings in the tobacco tonight*, he thought, worrying again that his kindness to mice might be discovered and jeopardize the possibility of Eva and Fifi being welcomed at the farm.

Meanwhile, Dal reached the porch. He hesitated at the bottom of the steps and then started up. He put his front legs on the first step and then the second. He pushed off with his one good rear leg and surprised himself when his back half was standing steady on the good leg on the bottom step.

"Way to go, Dal," said Farmer Frank. "You may not be a pedigreed Dalmatian, but you're one tough dog."

Farmer Frank went into the kitchen. Rusty followed him to allay suspicion that something was up and threw himself wholeheartedly into the food. Most of the bowl was gone before he remembered that he had intended to save most of it for Eva. He felt terrible.

Manny led Maia and her family into the house via the crack in the foundation. Alvin and Maggie were in their nest, and Maggie assured Maia's family that they were welcome to stay as long as they needed to.

"I recommend you build nests here in the house," said Alvin. "Food is always close by. We'll eat as soon as Farmer and Mrs. Frank go to bed."

"Thank you," said Linda. "We certainly appreciate your hospitality."

"We won't be staying long," added Robert. "We intend to find a place very soon, though I don't think it will be here in the house. I'd really like to find another rock wall somewhere."

"I'm going outside to check on Eva and Fifi," said Manny.

"I'll come with you," said Maia.

They found Eva and Fifi still hiding under the porch and waited with them until the lights in the house went out. Then, they joined Dal and Rusty on the porch.

"I left food for you inside the kitchen, Eva," said Rusty. "It's not a lot. Farmer Frank didn't put much out tonight." He felt ashamed for lying.

"It's all right," said Eva. "If I ate a lot now, I might get sick."

"Have some of this," said Fifi. "I can't eat this much."

Dal almost broke in to say that he could eat more, but he caught himself. He and Rusty watched as Eva and Fifi cleaned Dal's bowl.

"Can I sleep out here with you?" Fifi asked, looking at Dal. "I think I'm an outdoor dog. I don't like to be inside. It makes me nervous. Isn't the sky beautiful? We could watch the moon come up."

Dal was momentarily speechless. "Well, of course. That would be…Yes, yes, indeed… I mean, sure, watch the moon come up. Great idea. Did I tell you I have three wool blankets in my dog house? With two of us and the blankets, we won't have to go into the Franks' house no matter how cold it gets."

"That would be wonderful. It would make me feel really good to know that I didn't have to go inside a house ever again. Maybe when I get older, but not now."

"You two have a good night," said Rusty. "Eva, we'll go inside. There's the food I left for you, and there are warm carpets to sleep on."

"What about Farmer and Mrs. Frank? Don't Fifi and I need to meet them?"

"I know from experience that night is not a good time to surprise Farmer and Mrs. Frank—or Flora either for that matter," said Manny.

"It can wait," said Eva. "Did you say there was a little more food inside, Rusty? I *am* still hungry. A little food and a warm place to sleep will be perfect."

"In the morning," said Manny, "Maia, and I will be waiting under the porch. We'll help Fifi and Eva watch for the right opportunity to show themselves to Farmer and Mrs. Frank."

Everyone nodded agreement and moved on to their night destinations. Rusty and Eva stopped briefly in the kitchen for Eva to finish what little food Rusty had left in the bowl. Rusty tried to look nonchalant, but he was feeling guilty until Eva finished and looked up at him as though he were the most generous dog in the whole world. "Thank you so much. You're very kind, and your breath smells good too—like dog breath. I don't know how to thank you," she said and licked his face.

Rusty was too overwhelmed to say anything. He just licked her face in return and started toward the living room. "We could sleep on the sofa," he suggested. "It's even more comfortable than the carpet."

"I wasn't allowed on the sofa," said Eva. "Could we sleep behind the sofa?"

"Sounds good to me."

Out on the porch, Manny and Maia watched as Fifi and Dal climbed into his small house. "You go first," said Fifi, "and get yourself settled with your bad leg. I can fit into whatever space is left."

"Well, okay, I guess," said Dal. "I'm not a cripple, you know. It won't be long before I'm chasing every furball that dares enter the garden. You just wait and see."

He maneuvered slowly around to lie down with his bad leg resting on top. Now that the pain was almost gone, the leg felt as though it was normal, as though it would move if he ordered it to, but it would not. Fifi curled in next to him. Warmth quickly filled the dog house.

Maia and Manny said goodnight and ran around the corner of the house to the crack in the foundation. "In just one day everything has changed," said Maia. "Now my family is here, and they need a place to live. And two dogs also need a home. Do you think Farmer Frank will let Eva and Fifi stay?"

"I hope so. I don't think they're equipped like we are to live on their own. Dogs seem to need people to give them food. Fortunately, we don't need Farmer Frank's permission for your family to move in. We'll get the neighbors to help, and we'll have them in a nest tomorrow night."

"What about us? When can we get married?"

"I'm sure my mother has the details planned, re-planned, and over-planned. She probably has the whole neighborhood stockpiling food. As soon as we get your family settled, we'll have our wedding."

"It seems impossible that we could really just settle in for a quiet life after all that's happened."

As they sat, cold fell through the still air, surrounding their tiny body heaters like an ocean encircles a small atoll—a source of life and a threat to it. For the moment, they were warm beyond reason and safe against odds.

When they entered the crack in the foundation, they found no one in Alvin and Maggie's nest above the heating duct. "They must be in the kitchen," said Manny.

"What's a kitchen, and what's in it?"

"Food. Lots of food. It's people food, but some of it tastes good. I don't think it's as good for you as the food outdoors, but it's easy to find."

"Good. I'm hungry."

They climbed up the drain-pipe through the floor and into the cabinet under the kitchen sink. Tanya was sitting beside one of the traps, eating cheese that Alvin had removed for her. Linda and Robert were sitting right outside the cabinet, waiting for their son Gary to come back from the pantry. They had eaten little and retreated to where they could escape quickly if necessary. In spite of what Alvin said, they did not feel the house was a safe place.

To Manny's relief, everyone ate and got back down to Alvin and Maggie's nest above the heating duct without incident. Alvin began to lecture on the importance of building a nest in the right location, on the overrated dangers associated generally with living in a house, and on the nutritional value of various substances found in the pantry. Everyone was asleep before he got through much of it.

Throughout the night, the furnace kicked on with regularity. The stomachs of the newcomers struggled with the strange food, and nightmares danced through the nest on currents of warm air. Many dreamed of performing magic, of being Zeus.

* * *

In Zeus's palace, there was construction dust everywhere as workers labored on an addition to the palace. The idea had grown out of his discussions with Athena on corporal punishment and his gradual conversion to the principle of "time-out." But there were many miscreants who needed time-out at any given moment, who needed supervision in the execution of time-out, and who could benefit from a spiritual setting that might contribute to feelings of contrition. There was the need for discipline and enforcement for those who might fail to see the benefit of the prescribed length of time-out. There was also, Athena insisted, a need for positive reinforcement—a compensatory reward for pain and suffering, not to mention the humiliation. The result was what Zeus called "The Total Time-Out Theater."

The theater had a central dome that rose to a height three times that of the palace, supported by twelve arches to form a twelve-sided building, a dodecahedron. The interior of this vast cathedral of space had five circles of rooms. Each circle had 12 rooms for a total of 60 rooms in all. The outside circle had the largest rooms for the larger animals and the central circle had the smallest rooms. The rooms had walls and doors but no ceilings. The light for all the rooms came from translucent amber panels in the dome of the theatre. Their translucence let the light in but precluded the animals in the rooms from seeing outside. It gave the interior an aw-inspiring aura, evoking piety and penance.

Animals entered the Total Time-Out Theatre through an arched hallway leading from the palace. The hallway was large enough to accommodate any animal, but had an electronically controlled door at the end that descended from the top. Its sensor lowered the door precisely the distance needed so that the animal entering, regardless of size, had to bow its head as it entered to set a tone of humility and remorse.

When animals exited the theater, the door came down to require them to bow their heads again, and they were required to say, "Thank you. I needed that."

On the wall in each of the 60 rooms was a stop-watch set from a central control panel in Zeus's executive suite in the palace. The stop-watches were on the wall behind where the creatures sat. While in time-out, they were to concentrate on their misdeeds and not on the amount of time remaining.

Across from each corner, a camera monitored head movements. If a head nodded forwarded indicating the animal was falling asleep, an electric eye would trigger a prescribed electrical jolt to wake the animal up. Athena had agreed to this, because she had to admit that there were animals, such as cats, who could sleep through time-out without gaining any benefit.

The length of time-out varied for each offense, depending on what had happened or what had been contemplated. Zeus recorded the names of the animals and their misdeeds. He felt it was important to keep track of recidivism, that is, the amount of repeat crimes committed by the same animals. It would be the only way to know whether time-out was effective. Ultimately, he hoped to answer all questions related to crime and punishment. It was an exciting prospect.

Athena decided that each animal would be invited to unwind from the experience by relaxing with food, water, and juice. The food would be vegetarian, of course, and she disguised her tofu such that no animal might be offended. The taste she'd perfected was that of shrimp. A few animals had heard of shrimp, but no one had seen one. Everyone was comfortable with that.

27. The House-Raising

The eastern sky was only faintly graying where black had been when the noise powered through the still morning, crushing the air and sky, and rolling hard across the dewed grass as it neared. Everyone inside, under, and outside the house leaped out of slumber.

Manny awoke from his dream with a start. Alvin, Maggie, Maia, Linda, Robert, Tanya, and Gary sat upright at the same moment. The noise was bearing down on the house like an avalanche, vibrating the heating duct, deafening thoughts of what to do. Manny leaped out of the nest and through the crack in the foundation to see what was happening. Everyone followed.

Inside the house, Eva bolted awake. "What's that? No one will sleep through that." She ran into the kitchen and out the door before Rusty could muster a protest.

Inside the doghouse on the porch, Fifi and Dal were afraid to move. Fifi thought she should run, but where to? Dal could not run. The noise froze her to the warm spot on the blankets where she was curled against Dal's stomach until Eva appeared: "Quick, Fifi, we need to hide," Eva said. "Something terrible is happening."

"But what about Dal and Rusty?"

"They have Farmer and Mrs. Frank to protect them. We have no one."

"She's right," said Dal. "Take cover under the porch. I'll let you know what this is about as soon as I figure it out."

In the bedroom, Farmer Frank awoke in a daze, peering in the dark to see the clock beside the bed. "What time is it?"

"It's only 5:30," said Mrs. Frank. "What's that noise?"

"Must be the trucks, delivering the house. The work crew and the neighbors won't be far behind. This will be the biggest event around here in a long time. Put the coffee on," said Farmer Frank as he began to pull on his clothes.

The first set of dual truck exhausts blew smoke into the morning air from behind the chrome grille of a tractor trailer as its driver down-shifted to a crawl and eased the rig parallel to the rock foundation between the two rock chimneys. It stopped and growled contentedly as the second tractor trailer's chrome pipes belched black in the down-shift that slowed it to a stop alongside the first one. The last tractor trailer snorted, puffed, and shifted more often than needed as it turned into the driveway, blowing its exhaust high and leaving it hanging in stringy wisps of pattern before settling to an idle beside the second tractor trailer.

The young driver of the last truck nodded to the older drivers of the first two, but no one made a move to get out or to cut their engines, which continued to grumble from behind the chrome grills as they fed the six hungry exhausts, gurgling clouds into the still air. The trailer beds were as long as houses.

"Good morning. You boys are plenty early!" yelled Farmer Frank as he approached the first tractor trailer.

"Good morning. You Mr. Frank?"

"Yep. You're at the right place."

"Well, we've got a house to get under roof by nightfall."

A panel truck with four workmen arrived minutes later. One of the delivery trucks had a crane to lift the pieces of the house and lower them while the crew guided them into position onto the foundation. Air hammers and pneumatic wrenches were readied to nail and bolt everything in place. The crew knew the order of things. By the time Mrs. Frank brought out the steaming pot of coffee, the first framed end of the pre-fabricated house was being bolted in place. A dozen trucks with neighbors and their dogs arrived. People were watching and working, and mutts of every size and description also watched and happily chased each other in circles.

As the day progressed, Mrs. Frank could hardly believe her eyes as she watched the house go up. Farmer Frank and the neighbors were nailing the sheets of plywood against the outside of the studs to form the exterior walls while the crew guided the roof trusses and nailed them in place. More sheets of plywood came down onto the trusses to form the roof.

Mrs. Frank and several of her neighbor friends fixed coffee, lemonade, iced tea, sandwiches, and cookies; watched; admired; and gossiped about neighbors who were not present, though it seemed that every farmer within miles was there. Everyone helped, and everyone commented—all of them favorably.

The house rose with a speed surprising even to those doing the work. The rock ears became chimneys. The moisture barrier followed the plywood. And in the end, the roof was covered with tar-paper by the lights of a dozen pickup trucks and six trouble lights. The house was protected from the weather, raised in a single day.

* * *

Manny and Maia and the rest of the mice from the nest above the heating duct began the morning of the house-raising, along with Eva and Fifi, watching the action from under the porch. They heard the trucks' engines silenced and replaced by the peripatetic rat-a-tat-tat of pneumatic and hand hammers; the whir of winches; the thud of framing set in place; the yelling of orders and warnings; the exchange of comments on the weather, the project, and the conditions of life among men in the satisfaction and sweat of work.

To Manny and his friends under the porch, however, this ordered human activity appeared as chaos accompanied by a Greek chorus of barking dogs—a perfect stage, thought Manny, on which to introduce the two new characters in the drama of life on Farmer and Mrs. Frank's farm. "Eva, Fifi, run out there and pretend you belong to someone. Farmer and Mrs. Frank will think someone forgot to take you with them at the end of the day."

Eva and Fifi ran out from under the porch to the surprise of Rusty, who asked, "What are you doing?"

"Just blending in, we hope," said Eva. "Help us get acquainted."

Rusty made a few rounds introducing them to the dogs he knew until he saw Mrs. Frank emerge from the house with his breakfast. Eva and Fifi followed him to the porch in the hope that he would share.

"Well, look what we have here," said Mrs. Frank. "You two don't look like you're very well taken care of. You must belong to Mrs. Grimbelby. I see her husband's truck over there. That woman is so stingy she half starves everything, except herself. Let me get you some food."

Eva and Fifi ate so quickly, Mrs. Frank gave them some more. "I swear that Mrs. Grimbelby should be locked up for cruelty to animals. You two were obviously just moments from starvation."

Indeed, Eva and Fifi did not stray far from the porch the rest of the day, and Mrs. Frank gave them such an assortment of treats that they felt not just welcomed but honored. Every time she gave them something, she scratched their heads, and picked foreign matter out of their hair.

Watching this, Rusty, despite being thrilled with general developments, could not help but feel a little jealous. How was it that all these years he'd been made to feel that eating was to be done only twice a day and in strictly measured amounts? Now, here come these lovely interlopers and Mrs. Frank is feeding them every time he looks around? Still, he was so excited at their apparent adoption by Mrs. Frank that he wasn't nearly as upset as he felt he was entitled to be.

Under the porch, Manny was uneasy from the beginning as he watched all the dogs running about. Although they were preoccupied with each other for the moment, that could change. "It's dangerous to stay here. Everyone get back under the foundation."

"Who's afraid of dogs?" said Alvin. "Does anyone know how many dogs it takes to catch fleas?"

"It's no time for jokes. I'm going back to the woodpile to let mom and dad know Maia and I got back safely and make arrangements for the nest-building and our wedding."

"I'm coming with you," said Maia. "Mom, Dad, you get as much sleep as you can today. We'll be building nests tonight."

"Where can we build nests?" asked Robert. "Our ancestors always lived in the rock wall in the fields."

"And you still can," said Manny. "Right in the rock wall Farmer Frank built between his old house and the new one with the rocks from the walls in the pasture. Tonight, we'll build nests for you and for Tanya and Gary to use someday too."

Robert, Linda, Tanya, Gary, Maggie, Alvin, Mud, and Winnie climbed into the nest above the heating duct, but no one could sleep. The kitchen above them was an ocean of sounds and smells as Mrs. Frank and several of her neighbor friends prepared food and coffee for the men working. Maggie observed that she had never heard and smelled so much going on in Farmer and Mrs. Frank's house.

Farmer Frank had been so busy building the new rock wall, the chimneys, and the foundation that he had not mowed the pasture that lay between the house and the woodpile. It was heavily overgrown with weeds and grass. Even in full sun, Manny and Maia faced little danger of being seen on their journey to the woodpile and arrived quickly. Martha, Fred, and Shyleen were in the nest.

"We're back," yelled Manny as they entered.

"We've been stockpiling food for the wedding," said Shyleen. "Mom has all the neighbors involved, and everyone is coming. Can I tell them about the nest, Mom?"

"Of course."

"We started it as soon as you left. We lined it with some of Caressa's silk. It's deep in among the rotted wood by the ground below your porch—just where you said you wanted it."

"A silk-lined nest!" said Maia incredulously. "Thank you so much. I just can't believe everything that's happening to me."

"There was enough for Bouqueet and me to have silk nests too."

Manny remembered the conversation he had had with Caressa in the pasture on the night they had returned from Farmer Frank's with her injured leg when she asked if he thought it would be crazy to go back for silk. He had not understood it that night, but now he did. It was passion—not irrational passion, but a dream to do something no one else had done. "Maia will tell you all about how we got her family here. We're having a nest-raising for her family tonight. We need you to spread the word among the mice in the woodpile to help with it. I'm going to invite my friends Rachel and Gophericious to the wedding."

"Of course, everyone in the woodpile will be happy to pitch in with the nest-building," said Martha. "But when is the wedding?"

Manny and Maia looked at each other. "So much has happened so fast. We haven't had time," said Maia. "How soon can it happen?"

"We've stockpiled food. We just need to let everyone know the time. We'll have it in the usual place, the tree-trunk corridor."

"No, Mom, we're having our wedding on Farmer and Mrs. Frank's porch," said Manny.

"Don't tell me you and Maia are going to be house mice?"

"No," interrupted Maia. "We intend to live here in the woodpile—in our silk-lined nest, of course. But we need a different place for the wedding because of the dogs and Manny's friends Rachel and Gopheresus or whatever his name is."

"The Frank's porch is perfect, Mom," continued Manny. "The porch is just like being out in the fields—open to the moon and stars. But if it rains, we'll have cover."

"Well, it's your wedding. You can have it wherever you want."

"Whoever heard of having a wedding on a house porch?" said Fred. "The neighbors will think we're crazy and without regard for mouse traditions. No one will come."

"Don't be silly," said Martha. "All the neighbors will come—out of curiosity, if nothing else. The more I think about it, the more I think the porch will be a fabulous place for your wedding. Our own son, Alvin, lives in the house. He and Maggie will bring food from the house. We'll have field and house food. And, of course, we'll need food for a rabbit, a gopher, and some dogs. Shyleen, Bouqueet, we have work to do."

"Well, it's not just the food and the place that's a problem here," continued Fred. "There's the business about inviting other animals: a rabbit, a gopher, a pack of dogs? How will they fit in?"

"Don't worry, Dad," said Manny. "Rachel is an elderly and wise rabbit. All the mice will love her. Gophericious talks too much, but he's harmless. We can put him next to Aunt Agatha. Neither will hear a word the other says!"

"And the dogs are absolutely trustworthy," added Maia. "Manny and I might not be here without them. And my family wouldn't be for sure."

"I need to be going," said Manny. "It's all set. The wedding will be on the Franks' porch."

"And it will be tomorrow night," added Maia.

Manny was exhilarated and set off at a dead run for Rachel's warren. "Rachel, Rachel, it's me Manny," he called as he rounded the first turn down into her hole.

"Manny? What a pleasant surprise. And don't say I look great, because I know better. There's hardly any gray left hiding the white in my hair. But I'm still going, aren't I? Can't ask for much more."

"I came to invite you and your children to our wedding. It's tomorrow night. Maia and I are getting married on the porch of Farmer Frank's house. Dal and Rusty will be there, plus two more dogs. I don't have time to explain. I have to find my friend Gophericious. If you run with me to his home, I'll tell you all about him and the beavers who helped me get home."

They reached the fence-line just south of the woodpile by the time Manny finished his story and continued into the corn field in the general direction of Gophericious' hole, the one with the excavation at the entrance that the fox had made so that it didn't look at all like the hole of a gopher. "This is it," Manny said. "Wait here. I'll be back in a minute."

Moving cautiously down the hole, Manny called out: "Gophericious?" hoping he'd got the name right. "It's me, Manny. I've come to invite you to my wedding. Maia and I are getting married."

"Manny! What a pleasant surprise. You're getting married to Maia? A beautiful mouse, as I remember, though she had trouble with my name, didn't she? Well, no matter. I'm used to it. It's the lineage, I think. It's a burden, actually, to be of noble lineage."

"I'm sorry I can't stay to chat. Will you come to our wedding? It's tomorrow night on the porch of the Franks' house. There will be four dogs there, but they won't chase you."

"Four dogs? And they won't chase me? Are they emotionally unstable?"

"No they're not mental cases. They're my friends. No one will be doing anything, except having a good time, eating, dancing, telling jokes, and singing."

"Telling jokes? Well, that's a good idea. I'll tell some gopher jokes. Actually, the jokes are on other animals, but they're jokes gophers tell each other, if you know what I mean."

"Of course, all jokes are accepted. Come to Farmer Frank's house when you see the lights of the house go out."

"I'll be there."

Manny ran out to where Rachel was waiting. "I'm sorry I didn't bring Gophericious out to meet you. It's hard to explain, but it takes a long time to meet Gophericious. You'll meet him at the wedding."

"I'll look forward to it. Your wedding is obviously going to be unusual. I can hardly wait. What about the beavers you mentioned? Will they be there? I've never met a beaver."

"I would love to have them come, but I don't have the time to go back to where they live to invite them."

"No problem. If you tell me where they live, I'll send one of my children to give them the word."

"That would be great. The beavers have damned up a creek on the sun-setting side of the far pasture. Do you know it?"

"I think I was there once. Anyway, if all you do is hop toward the setting sun until you get there, it'll be an easy go for a rabbit. Consider it done."

28. The Nest-Raising

In the woodpile, Manny found mice waiting everywhere. "We're ready to build nests," they yelled. "And we're all coming to your wedding too."

"Just give the word, son," said Fred.

"Maia's story about how you brought her family back is amazing," said Martha. "Nothing even remotely like this has ever happened as far as I know. My great grandmother knew every adventure and brave deed reported by any mouse or remembered by their grandparents, and she never told me a story anywhere near this interesting. We're all eager to meet Maia's family. It's wonderful to have this nest-raising, so everyone can welcome them to the neighborhood."

"It's time to go," said Manny. "We need to cross the pasture before the moon comes up."

All the mice fell into step. Of course, there was not a mouse among them who had not been to the farmhouse. In some cases, they had only made forays there as teenagers, looking for the forbidden fruits of cheese and chocolate.

In other cases, they had gone indoors during a particularly harsh winter.

But whether their visit had been a quick run in youth or a few days or weeks forced by the elements, each mouse had a memory of the house. Each mouse anticipated returning with fear and excitement. There would be cheese and chocolate; there would be traps; there would be the smells of cat, dog, and strange foods. There would be remembered narrow escapes exaggerated well beyond what had actually happened, but so oft-told they were real. And there would be memories of those who had not returned.

Looking ahead to the lights in the house, Manny saw a welcoming structure, a nest for mice and cats and dogs and people. It did not look frightening at all. On this night, the light from the windows evoked warmth, food, and the memory of George in his panty-hose nest so near the pantry that dinner was as much served as sought. And of Caressa, of passion, of silk.

* * *

Inside the house, Farmer Frank flopped down on a chair next to where Mrs. Frank was putting away the last of the dishes, glasses, and pots and pans. "Can you believe what we did today? Got the whole house under roof in one day. I never would'a thought that could be done. Awful good of the neighbors to pitch in."

"You couldn't have kept any of them away. The least they could do was help out, since they were going to be standing around here all day anyway. Well, look here, the

Grimbleby's dog is still here," Mrs. Frank said, looking at Eva, who was sitting next to Rusty in the corner of the kitchen beside Rusty's food dish. I swear that dog was near starvation. I suppose it won't go home now. Can't say I blame it."

"There's another dog I've never seen before out on the porch with Dal."

"I think that one belongs to the Grimblebys too. You can see how skinny and unkempt they are. Whoever owns them has been too stingy to feed them properly."

"I'll get on the phone and see who forgot their dogs."

"No need to bother. I'm not sending these poor dogs back to Mrs. Grimbleby."

"What are we going to do with them, then? The younger one might not be house-broke."

"Well, she seems content to stay outside with Dal, so it won't matter. Mrs. Grimbleby probably messed up the house training too. No wonder they didn't go home. I'm going to give the young dog and Dal some more food."

Mrs. Frank picked up an extra bowl, filled it and Dal's bowl generously, and went out to the porch. "You're a cute little dog, even if you *are* kind of skinny and unkempt," she said as she scratched Fifi's head. "Tomorrow, I'll get the rest of those burrs out of your hair."

Dal pushed his head in closer to get a turn. "The rabbits aren't going to know you've only got three good legs," she said as she gave him the attention he sought. "Really, all you have to do is show up."

Mrs. Frank shivered in the cool air. She looked west to the mountains and far south down the pasture fence toward the tall oaks in which raccoons sometimes waited. She looked straight in the direction of the army of mice advancing from the woodpile, but she did not see the invading forces.

* * *

"The last light just went out," said Manny, as they reached the foot of the scarecrow with the furrowed brow. Manny had become so comfortable with the scarecrow's presence that he had forgotten to look up.

"There are four dogs at the farm," announced Manny. "I know most of you have never seen a dog up close and the smell will be a little overwhelming. But these dogs are my friends, and we need their help. They'll provide protection. We don't have time to sneak around from cover to cover while we build the nests."

The dogs and mice quickly gathered at the foot of the porch steps. Introductions went quickly, and Manny set about organizing teams. Maia's father, Robert, led the team to explore locations. Their task was to find passages into the interior of the rock wall between the old and new houses and nesting spots near the soil.

"We need a team to gather the nest-building material," said Manny.

"There are straw bales in the barn," Alvin said. "Straw is perfect nest material. All we have to do is carry it here."

"Unfortunately," said Mud, "I heard that a wild cat moved into the barn a couple of days ago and sleeps in among that straw."

"No problem," interjected Rusty, "I'll stay with you until you have all the straw you want. No cat is going to bother you while I'm on guard."

"All right then, Alvin, gather your team," ordered Manny.

Rusty led them to the barn. He had seen Farmer Frank open the small side door many times. He put his paw up and pressed down on the latch, surprised at how easy it was. The door swung open soundlessly.

No mouse there could remember having been part of a nest-raising the equal of that night, or, for that matter, ever hearing of the equivalent in mouse lore. Within the first hour, the entire rock wall had been explored and mapped for nest locations. A fleet of mice comprised a virtual train that freighted from the base of the rock wall to the barn and back, leaving a track of straw as bits fell from overstuffed mouths on the journey. The straw was piled at the base of the rock fence where another team of mice set to chewing it into soft pieces for use in the nests, and yet another team grabbed the freshly chewed bits and scampered through the passageways that led into the rock wall to the nest sites near the warmth of earth in the center.

Dal was assigned to stay near the rock wall, while Eva and Fifi kept a sentry's march up and down the track of straw between the barn and the wall with one eye on the sky and the other on the horizon. There would be no mouse blood spilled on this night. Zeus could not have provided a more perfect shield from harm.

To make the work go faster, the mice sang a working mouse song. It had the right tempo, particularly for carrying straw. It went like this:

> Heave ho,
> Come and go.
> No rest,
> Build a nest.
> Very nice,
> Homes for mice!

Well into the construction, Alvin took a few of the mice with him for a foray into the house. He knew that everyone would be hungry. He was hungry. Within minutes, the distance from the pantry to the base of the rock wall had become a conveyor of delicacies, topped, of course, by chocolate stars, which seemed to give everyone extra energy and enthusiasm for the task. The three nests were finished with material and time to spare, so they built three extras for future expansion.

Only a few finishing touches were left when Shyleen declared, "These nests out here in the cold need wool. Let's go into the house and get some socks."

"Isn't that dangerous?" asked Linda, Maia's mother.

"Not at all," said Rusty. "There's a basket in the Franks' bedroom that always has socks in it. I know, because I sleep near it and have to smell that stuff. Just one of the many compromises a dog has to make to get two meals a day.

Being a dog is not as easy as it looks. I'll show you where the socks are."

"I'll help carry the socks," said Eva.

"I'll come too," said Shyleen. "I know how to tell if they're wool."

Rusty led the way to the bedroom. Everything was normal. Mrs. Frank was sleeping content in the knowledge that she had saved two innocent creatures from the heartless Mrs. Grimbleby. Farmer Frank was in the deep sleep of tired muscles.

Flora was curled next to Mrs. Frank in a state of general indignation. She was not sleeping soundly. Two of the dogs had not gone home, and Mrs. Frank had fed them. It was obvious to Flora that they were homeless and of questionable pedigree. Homeless dogs could not be trusted to leave. They might move in and drive cats of proper breeding out—not directly, of course. No dog could force her out, but Flora vowed even as she settled in for the night that she would not stay. This was the last straw. She would move to a house where cats were held in their proper high regard and where there were no dogs. Not even one.

Shyleen, Rusty, and Eva entered the bedroom and immediately spied two socks lying over a pair of shoes next to the bed. "Strong enough to knock a dog over," whispered Eva.

"They smell the worst the first night. The ones in this basket won't be quite as bad," whispered Rusty, as he pulled the clothes basket out from under the bottom shelf of the closet and tipped it over.

The clothes tumbled across the floor toward the bed, where Flora was suddenly wide awake. The smell was too irritating. Rusty's smell was part of what always polluted the air, but now there was the smell of another dog. And a mouse! Flora leaped to her feet, her every hair become a quill, and let out a hiss that froze the invaders where they stood. On any other night, she would simply have threatened to attack and not deployed her weapons. But she was too tense from the anxiety and indignity of the day for tactics. Her rage was irrational.

She leaped off the bed without a thought to objective or strategy. Mid-air, however, the first target was obvious. She sent a claw straight toward the nose of Eva: that symbol of borders breached, of tradition and culture shattered, of home and hearth become an inn, where once a castle it had been.

Eva stared at the green eyes flying toward her and could not move. Rusty watched unbelieving. Much as he would never have admitted it, Flora was like a sister to him. He knew her well. They had shared the fortunes of the household for more than a decade—the good times and the lean—and had secretly sympathized with each other for the indignities imposed by careless grandchildren. They were feuding best friends. He knew this cat, and he could not believe what he was seeing. Flora was flying off the bed with a claw aimed at the love of his life. And it landed square on Eva's nose. The blood spurted before she yelped.

Flora was not finished. She landed between the dogs and flattened Shyleen under her front paws. Flora knew what to do with a mouse, biting it with the steel of anger. She would not release this prize for all the tuna on the high seas!

Rusty, however, also reacted decisively. He opened his mouth and closed it around Flora—not so hard as to break any bones, but hard enough to shock the both of them. Heretofore, Flora's threats to filet his nose at the slightest provocation had kept him in a negotiating stance over some issues and downright conciliatory over most. To the dogs of the neighborhood, he presented this as artful deal-making through which he prevailed by seeming to capitulate. As a result, Rusty may have been more shocked than Flora at the impulse that found her in his mouth. He dropped her. She dropped Shyleen.

It was Eva's turn to react. "Get in the sock," she said to Shyleen who was hurting but did not feel mortally wounded. As quickly as Shyleen was in the sock, Eva grabbed it and started for the door. Rusty grabbed another sock and ran after her.

Mrs. Frank pulled the chain on the light beside the bed in time to see nothing more than Rusty's and Eva's tails turning the corner in their exit. "What happened to you?" she asked Flora who stood in a state of immobile disgust dripping and stinking of dog slobber!

"What got into Flora?" asked Farmer Frank.

"I don't know. I guess she was upset about that new dog. I saw her and Rusty leaving just as I put on the light."

"Rusty's been sleeping in here for years. Flora never made a fuss before."

"Come on Flora. Come back up on the bed," urged Mrs. Frank.

"We need to find those two dogs' home."

"I'm not taking those dogs back to Mrs. Grimbleby."

"You don't know they belong to her."

"Well where do you think they belong? We can put a notice up at church and down at the post office, but if they belong to Mrs. Grimbleby, I'm not sending them home without alerting the humane society."

"It's been a long day," said Farmer Frank.

Mrs. Frank turned out the light. She did not fall asleep immediately and called for Flora to come back to bed. Flora was still stunned and nauseated. She could not bring herself to start licking off the dog slobber. Eventually, she rolled in the pile of dirty clothes, which removed the worst of it, and leaped back onto the bed. Mrs. Frank coaxed her next to her and scratched her on the top of the head and under the chin. "You've had a rough night, looks like. If we keep these dogs, maybe we could get a kitten to keep you company?"

Flora's heart almost stopped altogether. A kitten!? She knew that word. Even more dogs would be better than that! Mrs. Frank was soon asleep, but not Flora. She would be up much of the night, stewing over the prospect of a kitten, and returning her hair to its natural beauty, cleanliness, and smell.

* * *

Rusty and Eva delivered the socks to the waiting mice outside. Shyleen crawled out and explained what happened to the amazed audience. "Rusty saved my life."

"Well, I've put that cat in her place pretty regularly around here; tonight, she just forgot who's boss in this house," said Rusty proudly.

"Are you all right?" asked Martha, fussing over Shyleen. "You have teeth marks in your sides."

"I think so. The teeth seem to have missed everything important."

"Do you think people know mice steal socks to make nests?" asked Bouqueet as they chewed the socks into pieces for nest material.

"I don't think so. I think they blame it on the washer and dryer," said Maggie. "Mrs. Frank often looks around inside them as though something is missing."

"It wouldn't surprise me if they knew," said Alvin. "People seem to be awful mad at us. They don't set out those traps to show their gratitude that we've lessened their load of socks to wash. I think it's called the death penalty."

"I think they're angry about the food," said Bouqueet. "Mice should eat the food in the fields."

As work wound down, Alvin brought out a little more cereal, rice, raisins, and, of course, chocolate.

"I can hardly believe we have nests in the same rock wall—just in a new location—and lined with wool, too. It's too good to be true," said Linda. "I'm sure the spirits of our family will find us and feel at home here, too."

"Everyone in the community is delighted to have you here," said Fred. "And tomorrow night is the wedding, so we'd better get some rest."

Manny joined his family in Alvin and Maggie's nest. Maia joined her family in their new, wool-lined nest in the rock wall. Until they found mates, Tanya and Gary would stay there, as well. A nest without a mate is cold, even when lined with wool.

In Alvin and Maggie's nest, Martha continued to fuss over Shyleen. "Are you sure you're all right?"

"I don't have much pain. I'm just a little sore."

"You were lucky. I shouldn't have let you go in for the socks."

"I never felt afraid, even when Flora had me in her mouth. When I went into the room, I could feel Caressa's spirit with me. I knew I would be okay."

Martha held her, but not too tightly. "We all need rest."

Everyone lay down and fell quickly into the sleep of aching muscles. Except Manny. Tomorrow he would be married. From then on, he would have to be completely grown up. No more childish fantasies of magic powers when he, himself, would have children. No more invincible Zeus with a rod of lightning and thunderbolts, protector of mice everywhere at all times. After tomorrow, he would be with Maia, whose love and companionship he valued much more than he valued his fantasy. Yes, they would be married tomorrow, but tonight seemed perfect for one last fantasy: the marriage of Zeus and Athena.

* * *

Athena felt that their wedding should be a carefree day of happiness and joy for all mice, a condition that required a moratorium on eating mice for the 24-hour period of their wedding. To this end, she called together an assembly of representatives of all the mice-eaters of the world for the purpose of reaching such an agreement. The proposal on which she sought agreement was that on the day of their wedding, no predator would make an aggressive move toward a mouse. Not a single mouse would be eaten or harmed. Not one mouse hair would be touched.

When the moratorium was first presented, the great horned owl reacted with a long speech that began as a rationalization for carnivorous appetites, continued as an occasion for self-aggrandizement, and concluded with a pronouncement that the owls, in view of their superior wisdom, would spend the day contemplating the physics of flight and the optics of night vision.

The Persian, speaking for cats, waxed poetic on cats' aristocratic origins and revealed their plan to spend the day in personal grooming and luxurious cat-napping.

The snakes' representative was short and to the point. One day without food was no big deal for a snake. They would abide by the decision of the council.

The problem Zeus had with this was that the snakes' agreement was too easy. There was no sacrifice involved. Therefore, it raised the question of whether it was sincere. It almost certainly was not.

Nevertheless, as Athena pointed out to Zeus, motive is impossible to attribute to others. "If they do the right thing," she said, "you have to give them credit. Otherwise, the whole universe of values would crumble."

The hawk began by requesting dispensation for an all-out assault on chipmunks as compensation. On another day, this might have provoked a lightning bolt from Zeus's rod, but he had promised Athena he would not use physical intimidation. So, instead, he began by pointing out that the moratorium on mice was not a license to stuff one's ugly face—he let that little insult slip out—with the flesh of other innocents, but an opportunity to cleanse one's body through fasting. "You could feed on the flesh of road kill, for example," he said. "The experience might inspire humility, gratitude, and similar uplifting emotions."

"Don't be absurd," said the hawk. "We are not vultures! We eat nothing but the finest… I mean we need healthy, nutritious food."

"Never mind," said Athena. "Let's not get into an argument about suitable dietary substitutes. You eat whatever you want. It just can't include mice. That's the proposal on the assembly floor."

Athena had a way of saying things that got to the point. And without ever threatening to zap anyone, she got them to agree with her. It had only partly to do with persuasion; it had a lot to do with compromise posed as concession. Zeus was clueless in how to do this, but he admired it.

"So be it," said the hawk at last. "We will eat no mice on the day of your wedding. Instead, we will spend the day studying the thermodynamics of wind currents off the eastern slopes of the Blue Ridge foothills and the aerodynamics of drag coefficients in glide, dive, and climbing flight patterns." He sat back smugly in his chair with his wings folded and an arrogant look on his face.

The fox surprised everyone by agreeing straight away. "No problem," he said. "It is the great pleasure of the foxes of the world to declare a moratorium on mice-eating in honor of the marriage of Zeus and Athena. We fox are great proponents of mouse matrimony. Fox have been known to celebrate mouse weddings for days. Yes, indeed, we are delighted by the prospect of this union to produce more edibles."

Zeus raised his rod for a zap, but Athena reached over and pulled it down, whispering, "Motive is irrelevant. We have our agreement."

"Thank you all for coming," she said, addressing everyone at the council table. "You are all invited to the wedding, which will begin promptly at 10:00 a.m. tomorrow and continue until dawn of the following day. There will be abundant food—all of the vegetarian variety, of course. Please join us. There will be thousands of mice in attendance, and even the slightest transgression will cause you deep regret. The moratorium on harming mice is in effect for 24 hours, beginning at 6:00 a.m. tomorrow. Assembly dismissed."

29. An Historic Ceremony

Excitement built as the sun neared the end of its day's journey. The mice from the woodpile had stocked the food from the fields at the foot of the President Abraham Lincoln scarecrow, which appeared to take a personal interest in guarding it from crows and other feathered free-loaders. Rusty and Eva hid vegetables under the porch. Alvin removed the cheese from the trap under the kitchen sink, even though Mrs. Frank was still fixing dinner. Everything was in place; everyone was eager, poised, waiting, watching for the unsuspecting Farmer and Mrs. Frank's porch to be transformed for this one night into an epic wedding pavilion destined for legend.

At last, Farmer Frank appeared on the porch, set out food and water for Dal and Fifi, and walked to the far end of the garden where he lifted the Marilyn Monroe scarecrow up by the pole that allowed her to turn in the wind. He carried her to where the President Abraham Lincoln scarecrow presided and lifted him from his fastenings, as well. If he had looked carefully, he might have seen the mice hiding in the tall grass, barely breathing least he notice them in the last light of evening. He did not.

He carried the scarecrows to the porch and leaned them up against the house on either side of the new back door. "You're both looking a little the worse for wear. I'll fix you up with some new duds tomorrow. Brighter colors, so the birds can see you better. Maybe I won't put in a garden next spring, and you can retire."

He said that, but he knew better. The garden was a source of pride, and the scarecrows were a part of the history of the place, their masks a reminder of the night he and Mrs. Frank met, fell in love, and danced until morning.

As soon as the door closed behind Farmer Frank, Manny ran around the corner of the house and up one of the six by six's holding up the porch. He could hardly believe his eyes. The woman with the wonderful smile and the man with the stern face were waiting for him. The scarecrow with the smile seemed delighted to be part of the wedding. And on this night, the scarecrow with the furrowed brow appeared to put the cares of the world behind him to enjoy the event and add his blessing to it. The guardians of the garden would be the sentries for his and Maia's wedding.

"Dal," he called, "It's time to put out the blankets. The food is on its way."

Fifi and Dal spread out the pale blue wool blanket with numerous moth holes in it. Next, they spread out the faded Indian blanket that the Franks had bought on a trip through New Mexico. Finally, they spread out the army blanket that

Farmer Frank had been given by an uncle when he was young. The blankets covered half the porch.

Rusty and Eva brought vegetables onto the porch, and Martha organized the food: mounds of cheerios, raisins, rice, peanuts, and chocolate among the piles of corn, dogwood seeds, sassafras seeds, pear seeds, persimmon seeds, chestnuts, walnuts, and spicebush berries. The preparations were in order.

And then Manny saw them, a veritable phalanx of animals coming across the pasture from just beyond where he could see clearly. There were rabbits—quite a number of them—an animal the right size and of adequate energetic movement to be a gopher, and four beavers.

The introductions took a long time, particularly since Gophericious spent several minutes explaining his lineage, ending with a gratuitous statement about how he realized lineage was not so valued by other animals. This was followed by Bernard's lecture on the gift of structural engineering bestowed on beavers generally but on him in particular. He ended by advising the mice to build moats. "Generally speaking," he said, "water affords protection from a broad variety of no accounts that otherwise can invade your house and home."

Everyone listened politely, and some of the mice began to recite ancestor stories, as well. In the middle of it, Rusty found the opportunity he had been seeking to get a word alone with Manny. "I have a big favor to ask," he began. "Eva and I and Fifi and Dal would also like to get married. We don't need anything special done for us. Dogs get married by howling at the moon. So, we'll just howl at the moon whenever you tell us it's the right time to do it."

"That's fantastic. I'll tell Moses. He'll do something special for you, I'm sure."

Looking for Moses, Manny saw his mother sitting alone. "Is anything the matter?"

"Oh, no, I was just thinking how perfect it's worked out to have your wedding here. This house is where George made his nest and where Caressa found her obsession. The porch brings our world and their spirits together. And it's an absolutely beautiful night to have a wedding here on this porch."

Moses was running over the ceremony in his mind. He wanted everyone to leave feeling that he was the best, even though he was without competition in these affairs. There would be more mice at this wedding than any other; there would be house mice and field mice, new arrivals from a far off land, and animals that were not mice. So, when Manny asked him to marry Eva and Rusty and Fifi and Dal, he was completely unnerved. He had no notion about marrying dogs. "Are you sure you want to include them?" he asked Maia, hoping the answer would be negative.

"Absolutely! Manny and I might not be here—definitely my family would not be—but for these dogs. We're counting on you. The dogs have no tradition of weddings, so whatever you do will be special to them—and to us too."

"All right, I suppose there is a need for someone of my ability. Just give me a few minutes to gather my thoughts."

Unfortunately, nothing was coming to him. What do you say to a dog about working together to weather the difficult times? Dogs have no natural enemies. They are never in danger. Their worst nightmare might be a food dish filled only half full or filled with a variety of dog food that is not their favorite flavor. Moses was trying to think of an inoffensive way to refuse to marry the dogs when Fred announced it was time to begin.

Moses ran to the far end of the porch where a head of cabbage had been placed. He seized on the cabbage as a natural platform from which to address the crowd and scampered to the top of it. He cleared his throat.

"We are here to celebrate the union of Maia and Manny. No offense to the others here, but in view of our size, I will have the mice move to the forward-most rug here. Maia and Manny, please come to the front of the rug.

"On the next blanket, we'll have the rabbits, gopher, and beavers, and on the last rug, we'll have the dogs." Moses waited for everyone to find their places.

"Let us begin," he said. "Parents, siblings, friends, neighbors, and relatives of Manny and Maia: we are met here to join Manny and Maia in matrimony. Mouse weddings celebrate life, celebrate the bounty of our species. Each mouse union results in many more mice to bring joy to the earth. We are here to share that joy and to pledge our support to these young members of our community in their inevitable difficulties.

"We all know Manny. His adventures are reflected in the unusual congregation assembled here tonight. You are his friends. You have shared with him the struggle for life that has been both his and yours. Some of us might not be here without Manny. Manny might not be here without others of us. We march in an interdependent circle of life, of which this gathering is a mirror.

"Manny and Maia, it is my responsibility and privilege to set you on course. The two of you have already surmounted unusual obstacles in the adventures that brought you together. You know danger. Life's journey has unexpected turns for us all. Sorrow you cannot predict may rise to meet you where you least expect it. So, even on this day when you feel nothing but love and happiness, I ask you to share these small pieces of elbow macaroni. They are hard and tasteless, but in your mouths they will soften, and in your bodies, they will turn to sugar. Remember this simple elbow macaroni. Let all the tasteless and hard moments of life rest in your mouth before you speak. Give them time to soften, and they will nourish your relationship and bring sweetness where you least expect it."

Manny and Maia each took a bite of elbow macaroni, held it in their mouths to soften, and chewed slowly.

"Life is also good, sweet, happy, and sometimes just plain delicious," continued Moses. "To symbolize the sweet moments of life, I offer you these raisins, a fruit born of a juice-filled grape. A grape in youth is sour; in the full of its life, it is sweet. To become a raisin, its nectar must caramelize with the warmth of sun and time. Take the raisin's caramel secret with you that your life together may bring you the sweetness that comes of an enduring and loving relationship."

Manny and Maia each took a raisin and began to chew it.

"With the eating of these foods, you have committed yourselves to each other and your marital partnership herewith begins. Everyone, please join me in wishing Manny and Maia a long and happy marriage with many children and grandchildren. Let the celebration begin!!"

"No, wait," said Maia. "You forgot our friends, Rusty and Eva and Fifi and Dal. You have to marry them, as well. Everyone remain in place."

"Yes, yes, of course," said Moses. "I'm getting forgetful, I'm afraid. It's just that this is so unusual." Moses was outwardly calm and appeared to know exactly what he would do. But he had no clue. It just came out.

"Well, now," he said, as the four dogs looked expectantly toward him on top of the cabbage, "as you just heard in the ceremony I performed for Manny and Maia, I warned them of the hardships they would face. You will also have some."

"I hope not," said Fifi, "Eva and I have had more hardship than any dog should have. We went without food for three days."

"It was a rhetorical statement. I was just calling attention to the fact that hardships occur and one must mentally prepare for them. That's all. Please, let me continue. As I was saying, you may well have some hardships."

"Actually," interrupted Rusty, "Fifi is right. Dogs are not meant to endure hardship. It's against our nature."

"Please, just let me finish. I was speaking hypothetically, of course. No one wants hardship. No one expects hardship, and no one deserves it. My point is simply that sometimes unpleasant things happen that we do not foresee, that's all."

"Really, he's right, you know," interjected Eva. "When I lived in the apartment by myself with my owners I never thought anything bad could happen. I was fed and groomed and walked. But then one day, Fifi came—I don't mean that was a bad thing, of course, but the circumstances caused bad things that were not Fifi's fault really."

"Well, I'm glad we're agreed on that then," said Moses.

"Yes," interrupted Dal, "having a useless leg is a hardship, and that's not normal for a dog, only when we have to endure adversity, we do it well, don't you think?"

"Nobody does it better, that's for sure," affirmed Rusty.

"Please," interrupted Moses, again. "If you will just bear with me, we can get you married. I'm sure you will have minimum hardships and handle them well. I wasn't making a comment on the character of dogs. It's a ceremonial expression."

Moses could see his point was being lost. "Anyway, I have these macaroni here. I would like each of you to take one and hold it in your mouth so that you can experience how even a hard and tasteless thing can become soft and sweet. That's what I'm trying to illustrate as part of your ceremony here."

Each of the dogs lapped up a macaroni and swallowed it straight away. Moses decided it was hopeless, resolved never to perform another dog wedding, and continued. "All right, now we get to the good part—the sweet and happy part of our relationship. The raisins before you are a treat. Life has its treats for us all. In a lasting relationship, the partners value these treats and remember them when life is hard. You may each eat your raisin, and in so doing you are now married!"

The howl that emerged from Rusty's depths was that of a young dog seeing the sliver of new moon that smiled down on the wedding for the very first time. Eva looked at him and saw the finest howler that ever raised a cold, wet nose to the sky. With Dal and Eva joining in, four heads were pointed, eight eyes were closed, four spirits were freed by the bonds of their partnership in this refuge among the Blue Ridge foothills.

* * *

Inside the house, Farmer Frank sat up with a start. "What are the dogs howling about?"

Mrs. Frank did not raise her head. "They're howling at the moon, I guess."

"Do you think I should check on 'em?"

"You can if you want, but they don't sound like they've seen something to be concerned about. They're not growling."

Farmer Frank lay back down and pulled the covers up. There was a chill in the air as the house waited for the furnace to kick in. Farmer and Mrs. Frank curled up together so that Flora—much to her annoyance—had to shift position a little. She'd heard the howling too, but she refused to so much as raise her head. She had protected the house from dogs the entire day. It was somebody else's turn tonight.

"I brought the scarecrows in from the garden and put them on the porch. They need new clothes. Maybe they took the dogs by surprise. Remember that Halloween party where we met all those years ago wearing those masks? You know, you wouldn't have needed the mask of Marilyn Monroe. You looked just like her anyway with your golden curls and blue eyes."

"Next thing, you'll say I still do!"

"No, but I might say you look better than she might have at your age. Could I get away with that?"

"Maybe you should quit while you're ahead—if you think you are, that is?"

"Well, since you haven't said I'm not, I'm happy to assume that I am."

They lay still for a couple of minutes. "You're not going to try to find out where those dogs really belong, are you?" Farmer Frank asked at last.

"No. Do you want me to?"

"Well, it doesn't seem right to steal someone else's dogs, that's all."

"You saw what they looked like when they got here. I don't think whoever owned them was all that concerned about them, do you? Anyway, we're not stealing them. They just showed up and decided not to leave."

"Rusty and Dal don't seem to mind, that's for sure."

* * *

Not mind, indeed. Out on the porch Rusty and Dal were ecstatic. "Isn't this great," said Rusty. "Did we die and go to dog heaven, or what?"

"As far as I know, we're still right here on Farmer Frank's farm," said Dal. "I've still got this bum leg; I know that. But I'm not complaining. Life's good."

"Couldn't be better."

Manny seized the moment and climbed to the top of the cabbage. "Parents, brothers, sisters, relatives, and friends," he began. "Thank you for honoring us by coming to our wedding. According to custom, the rest of the evening will be devoted to entertainment, singing, dancing, and feasting. And to start off the celebration, please join me in giving a big shout for our friend, neighbor, and entertainer extraordinaire, the one, the only, Marvelous Maxwell Mouse, a.k.a., Triple M!"

Every mouse who had ever been to the house was stunned at Manny's recognition of a title they had carefully denied Mud, but they joined in the cheering. No mouse would be so small of spirit as to throw a damper on the evening.

And it worked. It was Mud's best performance ever. In short order, Mud had everyone cheering and laughing. He did mime, leaping from one place to another, representing several characters in a mime drama. All the mice recognized Farmer and Mrs. Frank, Flora, a fox, and an owl, characters executing futile and slap-stick gestures in ineffective attempts to capture mice, while looking ridiculous in the process.

It was a wonderful performance, and the audience's appreciation at the end was genuine and vigorous.

Mud bowed several times and left the stage to shouts of: "Triple M, Triple M, crème de la crème is Triple M," led by Manny and Maia, but with the whole crowd joining in. It was Mud's moment.

After that, the ceremony pretty much went according to expectations and custom. Alvin told several cat jokes, most of which no one remembered. There was: How many cats does it take to catch fleas? Every cat alive. What do you call a cat with no legs? It doesn't matter; they don't come when they're called anyway. Why do mites live in cats' ears? Because there's too much snot in their noses. It didn't matter that the jokes were not all that funny. Mostly, everyone laughed because of the way Alvin wiggled his ears when he told them. Gophericious told a fox joke that no one understood, but everyone laughed where they thought they were supposed to.

"Time to eat!" yelled Fred.

"Time to dance!" yelled Martha, twirling around and bumping Fred.

Pandemonium broke loose. Everybody attacked the food. Beatrice and Bernard started slapping the floor of the porch with their tails; Gophericious ran everywhere and nowhere; the rabbits played leap-frog; and the dogs resumed howling at the sliver of new moon that offered light enough for romance and dark enough for mystery.

Even the lines on the face of the President Abraham Lincoln scarecrow appeared to trace a smile as he and

Marilyn Monroe looked on approvingly. The porch had never born a more strange or joyous assortment of noise and motion. Everyone circled among the small piles of food. The rabbits ate all the vegetables and tried some other things that Rachel was sure would upset their stomachs, but on a night like this, did it matter?

Alvin organized more forays to the pantry for food that beavers and rabbits could eat. And Rusty dragged out the dog food bag. He had never done that before. He always waited to be fed, even though he knew where the bag was. Tonight, however, was different. Tonight, excess seemed perfect. In other words, a perfect dog night. Rusty invited everyone to share. The rabbits, beavers, Gophericious, and most of the mice dug in. Rusty, Eva, Fiffi, and Dal ate to bursting. The entire 20-pound bag was soon empty.

Among the mice in attendance, neighbors who had not spoken for several seasons sought each other out to exchange greetings. Everyone danced. And everyone sang. Mostly, they sang one song over and over again. The tune was easy, and everyone knew the words. At least they knew most of the words. The song was a favorite at field mouse weddings:

> No tale of fairy,
> All mice do marry,
> Prosper and bring you,
> Many children too.
> Sing a song for mice,
> Please do treat them nice,
> Give them lots of cheese,
> Some aged cheddar please.

Put out chocolate stars,
The products of Mars,
Some veggies and bread,
Or berries instead.

Whenever there appeared to be a lull in the party, someone made up another verse for the song. Rusty made up a verse about dogs. Rachel threw in a verse about rabbits; Bernard sang one about beavers. Gophericious led them in a verse that went too fast to be understood, but everyone sang along anyway. It was the kind of night where it really did not matter that the singing was not too good, or that the words did not always make sense and were not perfectly remembered. On a full stomach, even Moses was feeling better about how badly the dog marriage had gone.

As the eastern sky showed hints of morning, Rachel and her family bid everyone good night. Gophericious announced that he would be on the go, so to speak. Bernard offered to return any time they needed help to construct something that needed engineering skills. He recommended moats.

Rusty and Eva helped Dal and Fifi get their blankets back in the dog house. Then Rusty carried the empty dog food bag out into the field where he hoped the wind would catch it and destroy the evidence. His stomach was not feeling so good.

Alvin organized places for the field mice to stay upstairs in the house. The celebration had gone on longer than any in the history of the community, and there was no time for the field mice to get back to their nests. "Can you imagine the heart attack Flora would have if she knew how many mice are going to be recuperating under her nose all day tomorrow?" he said, as he led everyone up the stairs. "Fifty mice right under her nose and she not the wiser."

Everyone was staying at the house except Manny and Maia. "We want to spend our first night in our silk-lined nest," Manny said.

Martha gave them each a bump, and Fred gave them a final blessing. The hint of dawn was beginning to gray the black sky across which the moon had mostly retreated as Manny and Maia slipped out of sight. They did not run. They were in the danger zone of night and dawn.

At the woodpile, they sat on Manny's porch without speaking for a few moments, watching the day brighten, watching movements, slowing their heartbeats before turning to the path deep into the rotted wood to their new, silk-lined nest. Maia rested her head on Manny.

"I didn't tell you about Zeus," said Manny. "It will sound silly, I know. Zeus is an invincible mouse daydream I've had since I was born. I fantasized that I would attain magic powers and watch from everywhere, guarding all mice from danger, and punishing every creature who attempted to harm a mouse or even thought to do so. I was afraid of the dangers we face as mice, and Zeus was my way of coping with fear."

"No it doesn't sound silly. It sounds normal. I fantasized about being a famous singer. I thought that if I were famous, I would be so valued that no one would hurt me. Or that I would live in a world different from the one

I knew, a world where there was no danger. It was my way of dealing with my fears."

"But we will have children. I won't be able to protect them with magic or fantasy. I have to give up childish things. No more Zeus, no magical invincibility or lightning and thunder to protect us. Just Manny. Manny is all you get."

"Manny is all I want. You will always be a magic mouse to me."